ENEMIES

ENEMIES

GEO. W. PROCTOR

DOUBLEDAY & COMPANY, INC.
GARDEN CITY, NEW YORK
1983

All of the characters in this book are fictitious,
and any resemblance to actual persons,
living or dead, is purely coincidental.

Library of Congress Cataloging in Publication Data

Proctor, Geo. W.
Enemies.

1. Comanche Indians—Fiction. 2. Indians of North America—Fiction. I. Title.
PS3566.R588E5 1983 813'.54
ISBN 0-385-17654-6
Library of Congress Catalog Card Number 82-45334

Printed in the United States of America

First Edition

To Margaret and Willard Proctor, my mother and father—
a partial return for an investment made on a son

ENEMIES

CHAPTER 1

June 24, 1875

War did not end this way. Jess Younkin mutely stared over the neck of the sorrel gelding he rode, unable to accept what his eyes perceived. Sometime during the night, the world turned over, reversing itself so that it stood on its head. If that were not bad enough, no one had seen fit to warn him of the change.

Heavy Mexican leather creaked in dry protest when the Indian scout shifted the two hundred pounds of his six-foot-three frame to the back of his saddle. He slipped his right foot from the stirrup, swung the leg above the horse's neck, and hooked the back of his knee around a broad, flat saddle horn. Fumbling with the buttoned pocket of his buckskin shirt for a few seconds, he eventually extracted a dark briar pipe. From a pouch slung on his belt, he filled the bowl, battered and scarred from too many years of hard use, with crimp-cut Virginia tobacco. He dug into the pocket again to produce a wooden match that he raked across the sole of a round-toed cavalry boot. His cheeks hollowed deeply while he drew at the pipe to light it.

Normally, Jess Younkin reserved tobacco for a luxury, a pleasure to be savored quietly after a belly-warming meal, or to be used as a silent companion on nights he camped alone. Today, seated beneath an unforgiving summer sun, he needed the tobacco's comfort to help him sort through the thoughts and memories running through his head.

He pulled his hat's brim lower and studied the ragged procession that shuffled before him. *Wars don't end like this.*

He conjured visions of green-growing parks. Men and women, dressed in their Sunday finest, crowded around blaring bandstands. Waving flags and shouting at one another, children with pink-scrubbed faces darted among their parents. He imagined streets hung with banners, firecrackers, skyrockets, all blending in a joyous celebration that would dim the cheers of ten Independence Days.

Younkin sucked at the pipe, filling his lungs with blue smoke, then slowly exhaled. His head moved from side to side in silent refusal. He only fooled himself. Wars always ended this way—for the losers. Ten years ago, he learned that firsthand when he staggered his way across a Sherman-blackened South back to Texas.

Back to the pine woods, the rolling, green hills. His teeth clamped solidly into the pipe's stem. Back to find a wife and child he had never seen, butchered during a Comanche Blood Moon raid. Back to a state that had preferred to focus its military forces on an imagined Union invasion from California rather than protect the frontiers from savages within its own borders.

After the tears and a river of cheap whiskey that would not drown the sorrow, he dried himself out. The past nine years had been an attempt to ease the guilt, to correct the error of an eighteen-year-old boy who ran off to fight a war he held no personal interest in and left a pregnant wife behind.

Younkin's gut still knotted at the thought of his stupidity. The screaming crowds, the blood-stirring speeches, they caught and held him like a candle bug mesmerized by a bright flame. What had he known about cotton and slaves? His family barely managed to feed their own. Only the rich men in Jefferson, Houston, and Austin had the money to feed the mouths of black slaves. And states' rights? He still was not sure what that meant.

But he knew Texas, and he knew Indians. When he finally accepted those last two victims of the War Between the States, he cleaned his breech-loading Henry and bought a saddle and horse. He then signed on as a scout for the U.S. Army with its black buffalo soldiers to join the battle he should have fought in the beginning rather than following Jeff Davis and Robert E. Lee.

Nine years . . . now it was over. Younkin's gaze drifted over the scene stretched before him. There were too few of them to bother counting—the last stragglers, holdouts of a dead nation. He studied the gaunt, mirthless faces, the copper-hued skin drawn taut over skeletal frames by months of slow starvation. He sucked at the pipe, grateful for his own full stomach.

The braves came first. They held their heads high even in defeat. Yet something was missing, something that was not immediately obvious to a man who knew them as well as Jess Younkin. He leaned forward, staring at the warriors' faces.

That something was their eyes. Dark and dull, the eyes lacked the slightest trace of pride or defiance, a trait that had marked this nation the ignorant public in the East called the lords of the plains. The eyes gazed straight ahead, never moving to glance at those who gathered on each side of the procession to watch the final steps of a defeated nation.

At a distance of respect, the squaws trailed behind the braves, their faces hard mirror images of their men's hopeless expressions. Younkin could smell the hunger and fear as they clutched what few belongings they managed to salvage during the long trek from the Texas High Plains to Fort Sill in the Indian Territory.

There were no old. Younkin needed no explanation for their absence. Young mouths were fed first in harsh times. The old had been left along the trail to die in quiet dignity, their lives sacrificed so that the young might live to breed new warriors.

Worse were the children. The long, hungry winter deeply carved its cruelty into their faces, leaving them grotesque miniatures of their parents. The majority stumbled along naked at their mothers' sides, legs caked in dirt and grease, arms dangling limply from their bent shoulders. Those sickness and hunger weakened to the point their legs could no longer carry their bodies had been left behind with the old.

The children's eyes, half bulging from their sockets like the eyes of an insect, darted about, filled with fright. Still, they remained silent, even their footfalls mere whispers in the grass. No laughter, no complaints, no crying—no sound at all from their tight, small mouths.

Children? The thought surprised Younkin. He had never considered Indian spawn as children. He had seen too many companions killed by a concealed hunting knife when in a moment of tenderness they mistook an abandoned young Indian for a child. No matter what the age, size, or sex, an Indian was an Indian and would kill given the chance.

Younkin's gaze moved over the whole procession again. He sought within himself for some stirring of pride, a cry of victory. This was what he had fought for the past nine years. Defeat, utter, crushing defeat of the butchers who had taken his wife and child—this is what had driven him during the long days and even longer nights. He had hungered for revenge. Now it was his to savor.

He found no satisfaction. These emaciated remnants of a once strong and bloody nation did not evoke one murmuring of pride. Only a confused emptiness moved within him. That and the disbelief that nine years of bitterness could end so ignominiously with an incident that would have gone unnoticed had he not been at Fort Sill to see it.

They called themselves the *Nermernuh,* the People. The Ute tribes named them *Kohmahts,* the enemy, which early Spanish explorers mispronounced as *Komantcia.* Younkin pulled another lungful of smoke from his pipe. From that stemmed the name all Texians feared—Comanche.

For more than two hundred years, with bows and arrows, war lances, and finally rifles, the Comanches ruled a majority of the land known as Texas. They stopped the Spanish, the French, and the Texians from settling the open range and plains. They had driven other Indian tribes to the very borders of the state, if they had not killed them first.

Now they ruled nothing, not even the land allotted them under the Medicine Lodge Treaty of 1867. For that Younkin felt a sense of relief. The Comanche now belonged to the U.S.

Indian Bureau; Texas belonged to the Texians. He could go home again and attempt to build the life that had been taken from him when he donned the Confederate gray. The Comanche, the enemy, was no more, just another Indian nation confined to the reservation. The Blood Moon, the pounding hooves of mustang ponies at night, the war cries, the massacres, were now a part of the past. The Comanche could never rise from the dust they had been ground into.

No victory . . . only relief.

The sound of an approaching horse drew his attention from the Comanches. Sergeant Abe Potter reined a lathered bay beside Younkin.

"You were right, Jess." The black soldier pushed his hat back and wiped at his forehead. "That was Quanah Parker who led them in. He's the last of the war chiefs to surrender."

"Breeding always tells." Younkin smiled. The joke was old, but its irony was valid. The *Quahadi* band of the *Kwerharrehnuh* Comanche, the Antelope Eaters, was led by the half-breed Quanah Parker, son of the white captive Cynthia Ann Parker. Half Texian, half Indian, Quanah was the last to admit the end had come.

"They don't look right without horses, do they?" Potter shook his head. "A Comanche is born on horseback. He looks awkward on the ground."

"What happened to the horses? You find out?" Younkin examined his pipe. The bowl was cool. He tapped it on a boot sole, knocking the ashes to the ground.

"They ate them," the sergeant replied. "What with the buffalo gone, they ate everything they could get their hands on. Fish, birds, dogs, finally the horses . . . anything to make it through the winter. Even then, most of them starved to death."

Once it would have pleased Younkin to learn the Comanche were forced to eat taboo meat. Now, gazing on these pitiful stragglers who had survived the winter snows, he found no pleasure in the vengeance nine years had extracted. It no longer mattered, and he could not understand why it did not.

"We hurt them more than we realized at that canyon last

September." Abe swiped at his sweat-glistening forehead again. "Mackenzie knew what he was doing."

Younkin tried not to remember Palo Duro Canyon, a wind and water eroded trench that ripped into the Panhandle's flat caprock. If it had not been for a captive Comanchero, José Tufoya, Colonel Ranald Slidell Mackenzie would have never known the canyon existed.

Closing his eyes, Younkin attempted to shut his mind to those memories. It did not help. Palo Duro Canyon could never be erased. With Lieutenant William Thompson, John Charlton, and a Tonkawa brave called Job, he had been a scout for Mackenzie and his Negro buffalo soldiers.

Only four Comanche braves died in the morning attack on the canyon, but more than fourteen hundred horses were captured, along with a cache of supplies and ammunition stored for the winter. The horses had been the real prize. Horses, the Comanche's mobility, his measure of wealth and power.

After giving a few hundred head to the Tonkawas in his command, Mackenzie ordered the remaining horses shot.

The thundering rifles still echoed in Younkin's head, mingling with the screaming of the horses as they dropped beneath the hail of bullets.

When the final quivering spasm passed from the last fetlock, Mackenzie lit his torches. Tipis, food, clothing, buffalo robes, bows, arrows, war lances, rifles, ammunition, anything and everything left behind by Quanah Parker's band in their mad scramble to scale the canyon walls and flee was set afire. For three miles along the canyon floor hell reigned on earth while smoke and flame billowed upward to greet the morning sun.

Younkin took a deep breath to steady himself. That had been the last battle in the war against the Comanche. The ground had not been strewn with dying soldiers and braves, but with the carcasses of more than one thousand horses rotting beneath a Texas sky.

Now, a year later, Quanah Parker gathered the survivors of a winter's starvation and brought them to Fort Sill.

"You sick or something?" Younkin opened his eyes to find the black-skinned sergeant staring at him strangely.

"Or something." Younkin reached into a sleeping roll tied behind his saddle. His hand came out wrapped around the neck of a whiskey bottle. Pulling the cork, he slugged down a healthy swallow of the amber-colored sour mash bourbon. It did little to ease his unrest, only burned his stomach.

"Lieutenant Vardeman says I'm supposed to convince you to sign up again." Abe took an equally large slug when Younkin handed him the bottle. "He says Mackenzie wants you to ride with him when he heads north."

"The war's over, and I'm tired." Younkin corked the bottle and shoved it back into the sleeping roll. "After the Comanches, the other tribes will be easy. Hell, the Sioux ain't got the sense to fight on horseback. Only a total fool would get in real trouble with them."

"Then you'll be heading to Texas?" Abe asked, watching the scout nod. "Going to look up that gal in Austin? You know . . . what's her name?"

"Clara." Younkin smiled, remembering the dark-haired young woman. "Might do just that. Said she'd like to keep my company if I ever decided to quit scouting."

Abe laughed. "One powerful female, that one. The only person that got you to bathe more than once a week."

"Had me smelling like a rose, clean shaven, and hair trimmed close to the ears like some Houston gentleman." Younkin grinned widely while he flicked a hand at his shoulder-length, brown hair, then scratched a six-month growth of beard. "Felt like one of them fancy dudes when I was with her."

"Best watch that one. She'll have you clerking in her daddy's store before she gets done with you." The look of amusement abruptly faded from Abe's face. "What are you intending to do?"

Younkin shrugged his shoulders. "Still got some land in East Texas. Might decide to work it, or sell it for a grubstake. Thought about trying to join the Rangers. But with the Comanches gone, I doubt if there'll be much need of Rangers in Texas anymore."

"If I had any sense, I'd join you in three months when my time is up." The black thoughtfully bit at his lower lip. "Though I doubt you Texians would take kindly to having a nigger Ranger."

Younkin felt the soldier's eyes on him, as though the man expected an answer. What could he say? Abe Potter was good folk and a damn fine soldier. But the War Between the States had left a bitter taste in most Texians' mouths. And the fact that Washington had sent black soldiers to fight the Comanche did not sit well with those in the state legislature.

"If I decide to work the land," Younkin said, "I'll need a hand to help."

"They already fought one war to get niggers off white farms." The sergeant grinned, his teeth flashing broadly against the ebony darkness of his skin. "You know, I just might take me some time off in three months and see what's happening with you. I can always come back to the Army if things look poorly."

"If you don't find me in the Piney Woods, then ride down Austin ways." Younkin smiled.

"I just might do that . . . just might do that." Abe nodded thoughtfully to himself. "Which ain't neither here nor there. What I rode out here for was to give you this."

Reaching into a pocket, he pulled out a leather pouch and tossed it to the scout. Younkin hefted it in his palm. The metallic clink of coins came from within. He lifted a questioning eyebrow.

"I called in the markers owed you last night," Abe said. "Ain't much. Seventy-five in gold. But it might help if the going gets rough."

"You didn't need to do that." Younkin slipped the pouch into a pocket. The weight felt good. "But thanks. I'll put it to good use."

"Better than what the men would have done with it. First time they got off, they'd spend it on booze and whores." The sergeant's gaze returned to the Comanches. "One of them bucks has got something on his mind. He's coming this way."

Younkin looked at the approaching figure. He swung his leg from the saddle horn and shoved his foot back into the stirrup. *Can't be him.*

The brave looked familiar, the way he walked, the way he carried his shoulders. *Can't be. He's dead.* It could not be. The scout's eyes narrowed to slits as he squinted at the Comanche. It could not be. His man had been stouter the last time he had seen him—gorging himself on fresh buffalo while he rode away leaving Younkin staked out in the sun.

The brave came closer. Younkin stiffened. *It's him!*

"You know him?" Abe glanced at his companion.

"Black Hand." The name came like a curse from Younkin's lips.

"He's the one who led—"

"—the braves who killed my wife and child," Younkin said before the soldier completed his sentence.

"I thought he was dead . . . killed by Major Price in Hemphill County back in October." The sergeant's head swiveled to Younkin, then back to the warrior.

"That's what Price's report read." Younkin's gaze focused on the approaching brave. There was no doubt now. Despite his haggard appearance, the emaciated condition of his body, it was Toohmah, Black Hand.

Eyes locked on Younkin, the warrior kept coming until he stood by the scout's sorrel. He stared up, dark eyes wide and unblinking.

"*Tejano. Tohobaka. Nei mahrichket deta. Nei corre. Hein ein mashsuite? Hein nataes?*" Black Hand spoke. "*Nei nayoore. Nei habbe weichket. Hein nataes?*"

"What'd he say?" Abe asked.

"That I am his Texian enemy. That he eats burnt rocks, but still stands." Younkin translated without taking his eyes off the brave. "He asked what I want. What else? He lives, but seeks death. What else do I want?"

Again, Younkin felt Abe's gaze on him, questioning. A day ago had this brave stood so close, Younkin would have drawn his pistol and put a bullet through his head without batting an eye. Now? The scout shook his head. "*Suvate*. Nothing. I want nothing more."

Black Hand spoke again, and Younkin translated, "He says Texians are like black men, they walk without souls. He says we have been enemies for many years, that Quanah's surrender does not end that."

"Pay him no mind, Jess." The black chuckled. "He's harmless now. The Army will see he never steps foot out of the territory again."

Younkin nodded. Black Hand's words were empty, a last hollow defiance.

The brave's right arm shot out, his hand squeezing around Younkin's knee. A twisted smile moved across his lips as he continued to stare up at the scout.

"*Tohobaka!*" he repeated the Comanche word for enemy, then spat on the ground. Wrenching his hand from Younkin's leg, he pivoted sharply and strode proudly back into the procession.

Younkin glanced at his knee. A sooty handprint dirtied his buckskin breeches.

"What?" Abe stared at the handprint.

"The bastard's way of saying he's not licked." The dark imprint of a hand was the warrior's method of taking coup. Other braves used coup sticks to touch their enemies as a display of bravery. Black Hand's pride demanded more. He actually touched his foes, leaving his dark mark on their bodies. "But he hasn't won. Not yet!"

Nine years, the hate, the bitterness, sensations Younkin felt were buried only moments ago boiled to the surface. His left hand grasped the butt of his rifle and yanked upward. Before the barrel cleared the saddle holster, Abe's hand clamped around the scout's wrist.

"Let it go, man." The black's fingers dug into Younkin's flesh, cutting off the circulation. "It would be murder now."

Younkin wrenched his wrist from the soldier's grip. Freeing the rifle, he swung the weapon to his shoulder.

The distinctive double click of a cocking revolver hammer sounded beside Younkin. The scout's eyes rolled to the sergeant to find the barrel of the man's Army Colt leveled at him.

"Ease it back in the holster, Jess. He's not worth it. And I won't allow it," Abe said firmly. "Better I put a bullet through your arm than let you kill yourself this way."

Younkin's finger uncurled from the trigger. Hesitantly, he lowered the rifle back into its sheath. "Abe, you son of a bitch!"

"Perhaps." The soldier smiled, but kept the revolver aimed at Younkin. "Right now, however, I think it might be best if you headed south. It's time to go home."

"That's no guarantee I won't circle back and find him." Younkin lifted the braided reins from the sorrel's neck.

"No," Abe agreed. "But you won't. After you give it a good think, you'll realize no Comanche is worth it. Now, I think it's time you headed back across the Red River."

Reining south, Younkin nudged his mount to an easy lope. He smiled. The sergeant was a better man than he thought. He would have never given Abe credit for having the courage to draw down on him like that. Two to one Abe would have put a bullet through his arm if he had not lowered the rifle.

More than courage, Younkin admitted to himself. Abe had brains. He was right. No Comanche, not even Black Hand, was worth getting himself hanged over. The scout shifted in the saddle and looked over his shoulder to the buffalo soldier watching his departure. "Three months, I'll be looking for you in Texas!"

Younkin waved and was answered by Abe's wide grin.

CHAPTER 2

December 10, 1903

The snap of a dry twig? The crack of stones?

The sound woke Toohmah instantly. Yet, he did not move, but lay on his side, eyes closed, and listening. His motionlessness derived in part from a lifetime of caution. He could not identify the sound nor locate its origin. Any movement would give him away, and he knew not what waited beyond the buffalo robe covering him from head to feet.

In equal part, his stillness resulted from age. Sixty *taum,* the annual coming of ice and snow, had passed since his mother bore him into the world. His body no longer held the strength and agility of a young brave. It needed time to gather itself, to discover the new aches and pains brought with each sunrise. The night's cold breath, foretelling winter's approaching harshness, did nothing to lessen the nagging of his cramped arms and legs.

Old; he recognized the weight of his years pressing down upon him. The relative strength of his teeth, sharpness of his eyes and ears, were a deception, one he accepted to hide the truth from himself. The truth remained.

Few *Nermernuh* knew so many seasons. Better to have died with war lance in hand beside the companions of his youth. There was honor in such a death. Age lacked the strength to hold its head erect and proud. The ever quickening pace of years brought the slow draining of a man's mind and body that prepared him for the inevitability of the grave. *To be touched by youth once again.*

Toohmah's mind filled with memories. A hundred youthful faces floated behind his closed eyelids. He knew them all, remembered the feel of their names on his tongue. Names he neither thought nor spoke. The names of the dead, even those who died bravely, were forbidden ever to be uttered by the *Nermernuh.* Still, the faces, painted in black and red in preparation for a raid, remained vivid, as did the sound of their boasting voices.

Gone, all of them gone to hunt and raid forever young in the Valley of Ten Thousand-fold Longer and Wider that waited beyond the sun. And he remained to endure the shame and disrespect of age. The People tolerated the presence of the old, never accepted them.

A sharp crack sounded outside the robe.

Toohmah's memories dispersed in a heartbeat. Chagrined by the cloud-drifting of his mind, another sign of mounting years, he opened his eyes. A pale gray light seeped in beneath the edges of the buffalo skin. He slept later than normal; sunrise approached. The three days and nights spent in search of a medicine vision added to the weakness of his body.

Cautiously, he edged his right hand forward to inch the buffalo robe from the ground. He blinked, accustoming his eyes to the light while he peered into the coming dawn.

A smile slowly spread across the heavy lines of Toohmah's leathery, copper-hued face. A lone antelope stood twenty paces from where he lay on the ground. Apparently the creature mistook the bundled buffalo hide for a boulder. The morning breeze blew directly from the east into the old man's face. An unusual wind for this late in the year, but it kept the scent of man and robe from the animal's delicate nostrils.

For minutes, he studied the antelope's sleek form while its head arched low to graze on a patch of dry grass that grew amid the rocks. Its simple beauty pleased him. Even in the pre-dawn glow he could discern the wetness of its dark nose and the working of its small jaw. Occasionally, the creature's head lifted to search the land around it for signs of predators. Then it returned to munching grass.

A doe. Toohmah's smile grew to a grin. He saw the brown

of its large, round, wet eyes. An antelope was rare this far north of the Red River. And unheard of this late in the season. Had he but carried his bow and quiver with him. The doe would make several fine meals. Its wild, rich meat would be like honey to a tongue dulled by the taste of the white man's beef.

He suppressed the thought. A man who sought medicine did not come with weapons in hand.

Toohmah caught his breath. *Medicine?* Was the doe the sign he sought? *Kwerharrehnuh*, was he not of the Antelope Eaters, the proudest and fiercest of all the *Nermernuh?* Why else would an antelope awaken him this fourth morning of his vigil? And at this time of year when its kind should be far to the south?

He shook his head. Now was not the time to read magic into things that did not hold power for him. The medicine of the antelope, eagle, coyote, hawk, buffalo, or any other natural creature did not belong to him. His had always been the most powerful of *Nermernuh* medicine—the *nenuhpee.*

Many warriors of the People saw the *nenuhpee* when four days without food and water opened their eyes to medicine visions. Only the strongest and bravest accepted the *puha* they brought. Most denied the *nenuhpee*'s medicine, fleeing like a frightened child rather than accept the burden it carried.

The *puha* brought by a *nenuhpee* was unlike all other medicines. It carried a double edge for those who accepted it. Both good and evil might come to a man who counseled unwisely with the *nenuhpee.*

Many of the People considered the *nenuhpee* totally evil, like the awesome Cannibal Owl that flew the darkest nights.

For those visited by the *nenuhpee,* men whose inner strength and will could hold the vision to a true path, the *Nermernuh* gave the name *puhakat,* maker of strong medicine. A praise often bestowed on Toohmah in his younger days. Of the braves who rode with Quanah, only he talked with the *nenuhpee* and held their power.

His head moved sadly from side to side. Had the *nenuhpee*

not told him to shun Eeshatai, the self-proclaimed medicine man the Whites called Coyote Droppings, and his Sun Dance that brought the *Nermernuh*, the Cheyenne, Kiowa, and the Arapaho together to battle the Whites? The Sun Dance and its gathering of war bands did not belong to the People. It could never bring good medicine. The Sun Dance was the way of the Kiowa and Cheyenne.

Claiming to be a *puhakat*, Eeshatai gathered seven hundred warriors about him. Quanah rode as war chief to the People. Lone Wolf and Woman's Heart led the Kiowas, while Stone Calf and White Shield rode before the Cheyenne. Together, united against a common enemy, they thundered across the high plains to a trading post known as Adobe Walls to the *Tejanos*. Within that small mud-walled post were twenty-seven Whites. Twenty-seven against Eeshatai's seven hundred.

Toohmah closed his eyes to hold back welling tears. Before the day ended, three Whites died and nine warriors lost their life-breath. Many more braves were wounded by the Whites' buffalo rifles. The alliance of nations shattered and scattered in all directions. Eeshatai claimed a brave killed a skunk the morning of the attack and destroyed his medicine. But all knew him as a fool, not a *puhakat*.

By fall that year, the blue-coat Mackenzie and his black-skinned soldiers discovered the *Nermernuh* camp within Palo Duro Canyon. Then all ended. Eeshatai had led the People from their ways, and there was no path to return. Only the reservation and the twenty-eight years within its confines awaited the *Kwerharrehnuh*.

Toohmah stared at the antelope. No, she was not his medicine. But the doe was a sign, a favorable omen that told him the waiting was not in vain. If his body could contain its weaknesses, endure the lack of food, the night's coldness, the constant pipes of tobacco, he would be rewarded. The *nenuhpee* would come to provide the answers he sought.

His thoughts drifted to Quinne, son of his sister's daughter. The youth had seen eighteen *taum*, eighteen passings of winter's ice, yet remained a boy. Before the reservation, such a youth would have been blooded, gathered many horses, taken a wife, and earned the right to be called a man. The reservation and its soldier guards left no means for a young man to prove himself.

A week ago, Quinne, the Eagle, came to Toohmah's tipi. They smoked a pipe together, an action Toohmah would have avoided had he realized the son of his sister's daughter sought a favor. The sharing of tobacco bound a man to those needing aid.

After hours of sitting and pondering the correct words, Quinne agreed to Toohmah's insistence that the old ways must be maintained, that a decision would balance on the older man's vision. If a vision came.

Carefully, Toohmah rose, easing the buffalo robe from his head. The aged warrior's movement was imperceptible. Occasionally, the antelope looked in his direction. Her brown eyes perused the dark bulk of hide as though perceiving a change, but unable to comprehend the metamorphosis of rock to man.

Toohmah felt pride in his ability. A good hunter was patient. A man who remained motionless became part of nature, no more than a rock or a tree, as long as his prey did not catch his scent.

Past the doe to the east, golden-rose fingers of light reached toward a bluing sky. The last stars of a velvet night dimmed and faded. Slowly and softly, Toohmah filled his lungs, sucking into his body the birth of a new day. Its power and strength were all allowed him during the vigil. On this the fourth day of waiting, even the air held a taste much richer than when a man's stomach lay bloated with food.

"*Kwerhar, ein meadro.*" Toohmah threw the buffalo robe back, shouting for the antelope to flee.

Startled by his voice, the doe jumped three feet into the air. She landed on light feet to bound down the hillside.

"*Ein meadro.*" Laughing, Toohmah called after the fleeing animal when she disappeared into a clump of live oak. "*Ein meadro.*"

Pleased by his small joke, Toohmah turned back to the eastern horizon. Despite the stiff knots left in his legs from the night air, he sat cross-legged on the ground. The sun would be up soon. Little time remained to properly greet it.

He rolled the buffalo robe in a neat bundle. His palms caressed its texture for a long moment. Before the reservation, only the poorest of the People possessed such a moth-eaten hide.

Twenty-eight years had eaten at it as moths devour the white man's wool blankets. Yet Toohmah could not part with it. The robe was a link to the past, a reminder of a once-had-been time. While he lived, the robe would be at his side. When it was gone, there would be no more buffalo robes.

From a pouch beside him on the ground, Toohmah pulled out a pipe and filled its bowl with hand-crushed tobacco. He lit the bowl and raised it to the sky, letting the smoke be sucked away by the wind in an offering to the Mother Moon. He then held the pipe to the east and the fiery ball that pushed above the horizon, the Sun Father.

Bowl in hand and stem between his teeth, Toohmah drew deeply to fill his lungs with smoke. He held it a moment before exhaling. Steadily, he smoked the first bowl, tapped the ashes on the ground, refilled the pipe, and began again.

He followed the rituals required of any *Nermernuh* male who sought a medicine vision. His was the old way, taught to him by his father's brother. He shunned those on the reservation who used peyote to unlock their visions.

Worse were those who followed the White Warrior, an imaginary god patterned after the white man's god, the one called the Christ Jesus. Some of the People even followed this Jesus.

Their reasons lay beyond Toohmah's understanding. Jesus seemed a weak god who preached that war lances should be used to dig the earth and grow corn. Jesus spoke of love, yet in his name the Whites killed. What use could any have for a god who died with nails driven through hands and feet? What medicine was there in a dead god?

The Quakers who came to the reservation said Jesus rose from his grave to walk the earth again, then was lifted into the sky to dwell in heaven with his father. Was not the Valley of Ten Thousand-fold Longer and Wider the same as the Quaker's heaven? The old ways opened the path to that valley. Why should one follow Jesus to obtain the same thing? It made little sense.

Toohmah's gaze moved over the hill on which he sat. He had positioned himself on the rise's south face so that both sunrise and sunset would be visible. During the days, he waited naked beneath the sky, wearing only a breechclout. At night, the buffalo robe warded off the cold.

As with thousands of *Nermernuh* before him, he waited alone. He neither ate food nor drank water. The only things to pass his lips were air and tobacco smoke. It required a minimum of four days for a medicine vision to present itself to a seeker.

Four days; Toohmah whispered a silent hope that it took no longer. Seeking medicine belonged to younger men. While his mind eagerly anticipated a vision, his body could not endure more than four days without the comforts of campfire and tipi.

When but twenty-four *taum,* he sat six days in the summer sun before the *nenuhpee* appeared. Now, if answers did not come this day, he would be forced to return to his tipi when night fell. To wait longer would leave him too weak to make the walk home, he feared.

He finished his second bowl and lit a third. Today he would smoke bowl after bowl until he emptied his tobacco pouch. Through the tobacco smoke, visions came. He glanced at the leather bag. At best seven bowlfuls remained, the last of his monthly ration. A meager weight of tobacco with which to go in search of medicine visions.

He grimaced when he turned back to the sun. Aged, tobacco poor, his whole existence seemed against him. Only the weather favored his vigil. Rather than late fall, the air and sun felt like early summer during the day.

Even in its mildness, the fall had stripped the leaves from the trees that spotted the rolling prairie below him. Here and there, cedars and pines did stand proudly, displaying their evergreen coats. The only other greens visible were patches of grass poking through the browns and yellows of the fall range.

This once belonged to the People, this land extending to the mountains in the west to Balcone's Escarpment to the south. *Comancheria*, the Spanish and the Mexicans called it. In the Medicine Lodge Treaty, the Whites gave the *Nermernuh* almost three million acres in the Indian Territory. For a White with his farms and ranches the land meant a fortune. For the People who ranged the majority of the lands now called Colorado, Kansas, Oklahoma, New Mexico, and Texas, the reservation formed a prison. A prison the Whites tightened in 1892 by giving each *Nermernuh* but one hundred sixty acres and opening the remainder of their lands to settlers. The acreage meant nothing to Toohmah. While some of the People tried to adapt to the White way, he could not. A man could never own the land, only live with it.

Yet, even he, who adhered to the old ways, had been forced to raise cows. Their calves he traded for grain and the other food he needed. Better to eat dog and turkey than plow the earth, scarring her face.

He sucked at the pipe. No smoke passed through his lips. Except for gray ash, the bowl was empty. It felt cold in his hand. Tapping the bowl on the ground, he glanced overhead. The sun now rode at its zenith.

Toohmah shook his head. How long had the pipe been out? An hour, two? Age was like a swiftly running river that ate at its clay banks. Soon it destroyed the barriers that held it to its course and flooded the plain surrounding it to wash everything away in its path.

His tongue moved over his lips while he filled the pipe a fourth time. The action did nothing to relieve the dryness, the leathery texture of his mouth. He looked at the stream flowing at the foot of the rise. It would be so easy to . . .

He pushed the temptation away. He could not, would not, leave his position until the last glow of the day's sun faded from the sky. If the *nenuhpee* did not appear by then, he would drag himself back to the comfort of his tipi. He would quiet his thirst and hunger, then explain his failure to Quinne.

Another sign of his years, the inability to aid those who sought help.

Quinne would understand. Toohmah could imagine his expression, the unspoken words reflected in the eyes of the son of his sister's daughter. Where trust and respect existed before, the youth would view him with the contempt the rest of the young held for the old. He would be but an aged man who clung to the past, a remnant of a dead world. That would be the final humiliation, the final dishonor, to fail the last one who looked upon him with meaning.

Laughter like the distant tinkling of bells touched Toohmah's ears.

He pulled at the pipe. He contained himself, displaying no outward sign of his inner excitement. The *nenuhpee* could not be rushed. If they suspected a man eagerly sought them, they hid and delighted in tormenting the seeker. The *nenuhpee* came when it suited them.

A blur of movement flashed to the old man's left. He blew smoke into the air, suppressing the urge to cock his head to the side. If he did, he would see nothing. The *nenuhpee* were masters of masking themselves. Some said they held the power to change shape, even become invisible. Toohmah never believed this. The *nenuhpee* were one with their world and used it to conceal their bodies. Like a wood lizard, they blended with their surroundings.

Another flicker of movement—another puff on the pipe.

"*Cona cheak.*" Toohmah heard a small voice call the name his father's brother gave him at birth, Fire Lance. The name had all but been forgotten when the People began calling him Black Hand for his method of taking coup. Toohmah was a good name, one earned and one to be proud of. Yet to hear his true name was also good.

He sucked at the pipe again.

"*Cah boon chocofpe nertahmah.*" The voice called him an old man. "*Cah boon nahlap.*"

He did as directed and looked at his feet. Still disguising any outward sign of excitement, he stared at the *nenuhpee* standing by his bare toes. A warrior in miniature, the *nenuh-*

pee rose only twelve inches in height. He wore a breechclout and moccasins. His long, flowing hair fell in braids to his waist. Bits of silver woven into those strands sparkled in the sunlight.

Toohmah leaned forward and held his pipe toward the *nenuhpee*. The tiny warrior waved the offering away.

"*Nei tebitze utsaetah. Nei mea monach. Nei habbe weichket. Nei nayoore.*" The brave of the Little Folk stared up into the old man's face.

I am hungry. I am going a long way. I am seeking death. I live. Toohmah pondered the *nenuhpee*'s words, a riddle to be solved.

"*Nei mahnahichcah cin,*" he told his visitor he heard the words.

"*Hein ein mahsuite?*" the *nenuhpee* asked what he sought.

"*Coonah maheyah. Haichka sodishmedro?*" Toohmah requested the tiny warrior's aid in showing him the path to take.

The *nenuhpee* stooped to pick up an object from a rock at his feet. Toohmah bent closer to identify it as a small double-edged knife.

"*Voonet?*" the small voice asked.

The old *Nermernuh* nodded solemnly. He did indeed see. Silently he watched the *nenuhpee* slide the silver blade beneath his *wannup*, the G-string binding the breechclout to his waist. With a flick of his wrist, the small brave severed the cord. A thin, red line appeared on his hip. Blood. The blade cut the *nenuhpee*'s flesh when it sliced the binding.

Standing naked before Toohmah, the *nenuhpee* dropped the blade and moved his small hands to his barely visible genitals. From beside his penis, the most powerful of all organs to the People, the brave untied a medicine bag. He opened the bag and emptied it on the ground.

Toohmah bent closer. He eyed each object spilled at his feet. An eagle feather, a small bird arrowhead of flint, a tightly woven ring of buffalo grass, a string of black and red beads.

The old man sat erect. These were the very same objects the *nenuhpee* told him to gather and place in a buffalo hide bag when he was but fifteen years old! The same items still within the sack hung beneath his breechclout, nestled beside his drying testicles.

A cold shiver moved up Toohmah's spine. What was the tiny brave attempting to tell him? He did not comprehend the meaning. He blinked down at the *nenuhpee*, perplexed by the unexpected display.

"*Ka maywaykin. Ka pahrpee. Toquet. Ein meadro. Suvate,*" the *nenuhpee* said.

Not to kill. Not to take a scalp. It is all right. You go. That is all. Toohmah repeated the small warrior's words in his mind.

He closed his eyes to allow their meaning to come to him. His thoughts flitted like a sparrow that would not perch. Four days without food or water left him too light-headed to reason, to think. Later he would sort through what the *nenuhpee* said and showed him. Now he must do his best to memorize all that transpired.

Opening his eyes, he looked back down at the little one. The *nenuhpee* was gone.

"*Suvate,*" Toohmah repeated. It was all, there was no more to be said.

Rubbing a hand over his tired eyes, the old man turned his head to the sun. Darkness stared back at him. He blinked, then squinted, uncertain of the truth in what his eyes saw. Above all, stars twinkled like bright beads suspended in the air. It was night. He wagged his head in disbelief. The *nenuhpee's* medicine was strong. Time twisted in the presence of the Little Folk.

Toohmah placed the pipe he still held into the tobacco pouch and securely tied it within. He uncrossed his legs. They screamed in protest, knotting and cramping from being in one position all day. He grunted in disgust; he cursed his age, then rubbed the muscles of his calves and thighs until the knots relaxed.

Using his arms, he pushed from the ground to stand on less than steady legs. Warily, he lifted the buffalo robe and wrapped it about his nakedness to cut the growing night chill.

For a moment, he remembered the clear, running stream that flowed at the foot of the hill. It would be easy to walk there and drink deeply before he returned to his tipi.

Old rituals demanded that a brave be within his own tipi before either eating or drinking. With a heavy sigh, Toohmah began the five miles to his home, wishing a horse awaited him below. Five miles was a long journey for old legs.

When he awoke two mornings later, Quinne sat across a neatly kept fire from him. The young man looked wide awake and expectant. Toohmah studied the son of his sister's daughter while Quinne ladled a bowl of hot cereal and venison from a pot hung above the fire. The old man gave his silent approval. Quinne was a true member of the *Nermernuh*.

Erect, Quinne stood five and a half feet. He displayed a wide, deep chest when he handed the full bowl to Toohmah. "Water?"

The older man nodded and accepted a turtle-shell cup. He could see his sister's face in Quinne's features. The aquiline nose, the eyes dark and bright, the thin lips, the shining copper of his skin, told of the ancestry coursing through the youth's veins. His countenance was intelligent, unlike many of the reservation *Nermernuh* who carried the blood of other nations in their bodies.

Between fingerfuls of the cereal and venison, Toohmah's attention drifted back to the young man. Quinne's facial hair, like his own, was nonexistent. Even the eyebrows had been plucked. Many of the young men cut their hair in the manner of the Whites. Quinne's hair grew long and straight.

Toohmah saw the anticipation in the youth's face while he ate. But Quinne held his tongue, waiting in respect for the brother of his mother's mother to speak. That was good. Patience gave a man time to observe and learn.

Pondering his words, Toohmah slowly emptied the bowl and downed the water. Such a breakfast was not fit for a man. He hungered to again taste the richness of buffalo, hot and dripping grease from a blazing fire. No *Nermernuh* would taste buffalo again. The white butchers had seen to that.

"There was a vision." Toohmah stared across the fire at Quinne. "But like this meal, which sits heavy in my stomach, my brain has yet to digest its meaning."

The young man nodded, but did not speak.

"Wait outside," Toohmah motioned to the tipi's flap with a hand. "I will call you when the medicine makes its meaning clear to me."

"I shall wait, even though a year passes before you utter my name, Uncle." Quinne's voice contained solemn respect for the vision.

Toohmah smiled while he watched the youth leave. He then turned his thoughts to the *nenuhpee*. Time and again, he sifted the events through his mind. He recalled each minute detail, the way the small warrior held his body, every nuance of his tiny voice.

Gradually, the vision opened to him. The *nenuhpee*'s first words were not a riddle, but a description of Toohmah himself. They told of the journey he considered—must take.

The double-edged knife warned of hidden dangers concealed within all medicine brought by the Little Folk. There was good, but there was evil for those who could not control it. Thus the drawing of blood when the small brave cut his *wannup*.

The emptying of the medicine bag took longer for Toohmah to grasp. A medicine bag protected the man who wore it from the evils in the world. To cut it from one's body and expose its contents destroyed its power.

Perhaps he knew the meaning from the beginning but could not accept what the *nenuhpee* implied. He was not certain. But now he accepted. He was to carry no medicine bag on his journey. What must be done must be done totally under his own power. There would be no supernatural spirits to aid him.

However, the *nenuhpee* did offer him a key to success. He must neither kill nor take scalps. If he violated this warning, he would be unable to control the vision, and evil would befall him.

Toohmah gazed into the fire's dancing flames. The burden

was heavy. He sought medicine to make himself invulnerable for the journey and found himself abandoned by the Little Folk who guided his life.

Still, if he heeded the *nenuhpee*'s words of caution, he could succeed.

Heaving a long sigh, Toohmah rose. Reaching beneath his breechclout, he untied the sack hung beside his penis. He opened the bag and sprinkled its contents on the fire. The sack itself followed.

He then seated himself on the floor of the tipi and watched the flames consume the medicine that had protected him all the days of manhood. He could not suppress the chill that sent gooseflesh rippling over his body. He now walked alone. His survival depended on his skill and his skill alone.

When the last of the medicine bag dissolved in powdery ash, he summoned Quinne. The youth entered and took his position opposite Toohmah.

"Does the wind still blow from the southeast?" the older man asked.

"As it has for the past two days," Quinne replied.

"It is good. The wind will bring clouds up from the great waters in the south. They will be fat with rain and cover the moon," Toohmah said. "It will be a good time to make a journey."

Quinne's eyes widened, but he did not speak.

"Tell your companions on the second night of the rains I will lead them from the reservation," Toohmah continued. "I will have further instruction when I have thought on this matter further."

"I shall tell them," Quinne said, unable to hide his pleasure. "They will listen with open ears to your instructions."

"And tell them I shall not kill when we ride. My time for that is passed." Toohmah closed his eyes, recalling the *nenuhpee*'s warning. "Go tell them, Quinne."

The youth rose and left him alone within the silence of the tipi.

CHAPTER 3

December 16, 1903

For the second day the rain fell. Rain bred of icy arctic winds that swept down from Canada, across the northern prairies to mate with warm, moisture-laden air gently rolling upward from the Gulf of Mexico.

The first day it deluged the land in violent, wind-lashed torrents that swelled streams and rivers with flash floods. To the east, dark funnels dipped to the earth venting their tornadic fury as they skirted the reservation.

On the second morning, the storm's anger subsided. Through the day, gray and shadowless from the unbroken overcast, the rain fell with a monotonous constancy.

Toohmah sat on the floor of his tipi listening. The downfall pelted the walls around him, striking the stretched hide like a thousand small hammers on the skin of a drum. The lulling rhythm would have easily brought restful sleep had it not been for the journey ahead and the three men seated about the small fire with him.

The old *Nermernuh* drew deeply from the pipe and passed it to Quinne. The tobacco ritual both calmed the spirit and bound the four together for what must be done.

Toohmah quietly studied the three young men. Following his directions, all wore white men's clothing, dark and unadorned with the bright colors that so pleased the eyes. Their gazes moved slowly about the interior of the tipi to linger on the many patches that mended the walls. He detected the doubt on their faces as though they expected the skin to give way any moment and admit the rain. Inwardly, he smiled. His tipi remained warm and secure after many of the shelters built by white settlers lay in muddy ruins.

"What do we do now, *chocofpevista*?" The one named Chana called him old man. Toohmah cringed at the sound. The youth displayed rudeness to speak while the pipe still burned. He ignored the words.

Chana's lips parted to speak again, but Quinne placed a hand on his shoulder to quiet his companion. "He meant no disrespect, Uncle. Unlike you, we have never ventured beyond the reservation. We grow restless."

And nervous, Toohmah thought. A disquieting sensation writhed like a snake through his chest. His own nervousness? His own doubt? Of himself, or of these three he would lead south across the Red River into the land the Whites called Texas?

Toohmah nodded, accepting the apology. Their faces were brightly lit by the flames. Yet, what did he know of them?

Quinne was the youngest. Like the *Nermernuh* he was, he yearned for the adventure of the trail, to behold the lands that once belonged to his father's father. Toohmah did not question him. Quinne would do all required of him without hesitation.

Moreover, Quinne understood the full weight of the white man's yoke. At age twelve, he had been held and forced to watch four drunken soldiers repeatedly rape his mother and older sister. No shame lay in the violation of a woman's body. If a child resulted, it would have been accepted and loved as one of the People. A child was a child, to be cared for and nurtured no matter who the father or mother was.

Quinne's shame came in his being denied revenge. Before the reservation, he would have sought each of the soldiers and left them staked out in the summer sun, eyelids cut from the faces. Or worse, placed them in the hands of the band's women. Death from braves came quickly. Squaws could keep an enemy captive alive a week, screaming his every waking moment.

To be sure, the four soldiers had been apprehended and

court-martialed. Their punishment was to be sent to the white man's prison. After two years they walked free.

The penalty was not enough, if indeed they ever had been locked behind prison bars. What assurance did any *Nermernuh* have that the Whites punished their own? The four were taken north to a land called Kansas. Perhaps they were set free there? No *Nermernuh* could be certain.

Toohmah knew the one called Chana. One glance at the nineteen-year-old youth and it was easy to understand where he got his name, why his family called him Hog. Chana's nose lay wide and pressed flat against his face. His eyes were small and nervous, his cheeks fat and round. He stood two inches shorter than Quinne. The fat rounding his body gave him the appearance of a smaller man. Even his voice came piglike from his mouth in short, snortlike bursts. He wore his dark hair cropped short in the manner of the Whites.

The one called Boisa Pah bothered Toohmah. He did not like the twenty-year-old's name. Crazy Water was ominous. A man should not be named after whiskey.

Nermernuh blood ran in Boisa Pah's veins. His angular face revealed that. But the young man was taller than most of the People. Toohmah estimated his height at six feet. His body was lean and angular to the point of being lanky. His eyes were mere slits that shifted constantly. Cheyenne blood? White? Toohmah could not be certain. Like Chana, Boisa Pah cut his hair close to the scalp.

He knew neither Chana nor Boisa Pah's reasons for wanting to break the white man's bonds. Nor did he care. He would give the son of his sister's daughter a taste of the freedom the *Nermernuh* once held.

Toohmah took a deep breath and admitted the truth to himself. The journey was not for Quinne. He went for one reason only—himself. The Valley of Ten Thousand-fold Longer and Wider lay in the near future for him. At times its features seemed distinct and clear. Before he joined dead friends, who must never be named, he wished to visit the plains of the *Kwerharrehnuh* again. He wanted to touch the soil of the land the Spaniards called *Llano Estacado,* the

Staked Plains. He wanted his feet to feel the earth he once knew as home.

It was an old man's dream; one these three provided the means to secure. Their reasons for fleeing the reservation did not concern him. Each man must seek what he must seek. Toohmah accepted and understood his reasons for leaving.

"I must prepare for our journey." Toohmah pushed to his feet. "You should eat. We will be deep into the lands below the Red River before we rest again. But eat only enough to warm your bellies. I do not want you heavy with food. We leave when the sun sets."

Ducking outside the tipi, the old *Nermernuh* turned his face to the dark, gray sky. Large, cold drops splattered over his skin. He shivered. Was it the damp chill or his own nervous hesitation? Better to believe his trembling came from the weather than doubt himself. He tried to forget that twenty-eight years had passed since he last rode the trails of the People.

His steps were heavy as he walked to the dark trunk of a live oak five hundred paces behind his tipi. Carefully, he examined each step. The footprints vanished within seconds on the spongy ground. He gave his silent approval. Tracking them would be difficult in this weather.

He knelt beside the tree and used his hands to dig into the rain-softened dirt. Half a foot down, he found the oiled-leather bundle he sought. He stared at it a long, wistful moment. He had buried the bundle to protect it from grease and women during their monthly time of blood. Both destroyed the medicine it held. His efforts had been in vain. No medicine, good or evil, remained. The *nenuhpee* had taken that.

Brushing dirt and mud from the oiled leather, he stood and started back to the tipi. His steps felt strange. Another reminder that the supernatural powers had abandoned him. His loins seemed empty and lonely without the medicine bag nestled beside his testicles. A few days was not enough to accustom himself to the loss of something he had carried forty-five years.

Within the tipi, his three young companions sat eating a

light meal of dried beef and *tosi tothteeah*, a flat, white bread the Mexicans called tortilla. Toohmah accepted a portion of the meal from Quinne. His teeth gnawed a bite from the hard, salty meat, then chewed slowly to soften it before swallowing.

"The meal is dry, old man." Boisa Pah reached into a back pocket and produced a flat bottle sloshing with amber liquid. "This should aid your chewing."

"No whiskey." Toohmah shook his head sternly. "It is not a time to celebrate or relax. Whiskey will fog your mind. But carry it. There will be time for celebration when we have crossed the Red River."

Boisa Pah slammed the half-removed cork back into the mouth of the bottle. He glared at Toohmah, but did not speak when he slid the whiskey back into his pocket.

The old *Nermernuh* weighed his reaction. He considered ordering him to leave the bottle, but decided against it. The false summer had passed. If the rain continued, it could easily turn to ice or snow. Whiskey would help warm their bellies. Divided among four, there was not enough in the small bottle to affect their minds.

Finishing his meal, Toohmah lifted the bundle to his lap. He unwrapped the layers of leather to reveal a brightly painted war shield. He sensed the others' eyes on him when he placed the shield upon the fire. He ignored their unspoken questions, his total attention on the flames that licked at the buffalo-hide shield. The circle of dried skin darkened, blackened, then split open. The paper stuffed within the shield caught fire.

An amused, ironic smile touched the old brave's lips. The paper came from five books, each bearing the title *Holy Bible*. He had traded two ponies for the books to a band of Honey Eaters who received them from Quaker missionaries during one of the multitude of peace councils with the Whites.

The People's interest in books astonished the Whites until they learned the pages were used to stuff shields. Paper was more effective than dry grass and feathers the *Nermernuh* shield makers used prior to the white man's coming. Very few rifle bullets penetrated a paper-stuffed shield. Those that did pierce the shield's face were normally deflected by the mass of paper.

"My lance . . . bow and arrows." Toohmah motioned to Quinne.

The youth rose to retrieve the weapons from where they hung above the old man's bed. He handed them to Toohmah, then returned to his place by the fire.

Three pairs of eyes on him, Toohmah placed the bow and arrows within his buffalo robe, then wrapped all in the oiled leather that had protected the shield. The leather would keep the rain from destroying the old robe or warping the wooden bow and arrows.

Toohmah then lifted the war lance. After all the years, it still felt right in his hands. He could shoot a bow, pistol, and rifle. But the lance was his chosen weapon. It was honored by the *Nermernuh*. The lance meant hand-to-hand combat. The warrior who carried one never retreated. He had felt twenty-five men die on the head of this lance.

Fifty men and women, Indian and White, he had killed before coming to the reservation. Yet they did not bring the honor that came when the People sang his name for the coup he took. Even a squaw could kill, but a brave's courage was measured by the coup he counted.

He grasped the ends of the lance and bent it over a knee until the cured wood snapped in two. Each of these pieces he broke again. He placed them atop the fire. Inwardly, he wept. The shield and lance were old friends meant to rest beside him in the grave. But they were too conspicuous. The color of his skin and the features of his face would be enough to contend with on the journey. The weapons would be too obvious to any he met on the trail.

Rising, the old *Nermernuh* stepped to his bed and the clothes laid out there. Atop his breechclout, leggings, and moccasins, he dressed in black pants and shirt, purchased at the reservation store. He gathered his braided hair atop his head and stuffed it beneath a high-crowned hat. He would have covered his feet in boots had he the money to buy them.

He slipped a white man's belt through the loops of the

pants, then attached a knife in an unadorned sheath to the belt. The clothes made him uncomfortable, but he endured them. At a distance, they would appear White. A necessary deception for four *Nermernuh* to ride through the Whites' land unnoticed.

"It is time to leave." Toohmah turned back to his young companions. "It will be dark soon. We have a long walk before us, and an even longer distance to travel before the sun brings a new day."

"Where are we going, old man?" Chana faced Toohmah, hands resting impatiently on his hips.

"To steal the horses we need." Pride touched the old brave's words. The best horses were those stolen from an enemy.

"Where can we get horses?" Chana asked. "None of our people, or any of the other nations, is allowed mounts. Only the soldiers have horses."

"Listen to your own words, Chana." A thin smile moved over Toohmah's lips.

"The soldiers? Has your mind fled you, old man?" Chana protested, his eyes darting to his companions for support. "The soldiers have guns. All we have are knives!"

"And the night and the rain," Toohmah answered. "No more is needed. They are enough."

"I don't know." Chana shook his piglike head. "I didn't bargain on the soldiers. I want to ride south, but—"

"There will be no shame if you stay behind," Boisa Pah said with a twisted little grin that mocked his friend's hesitancy.

Chana glanced at Quinne. The younger man nodded. "One should not go if he feels uneasy about the outcome."

Chana's head swiveled back to the grinning Boisa Pah. The fat youth swallowed, his gaze uncertain where to alight. "I am not a frightened child. I shall come with you."

A grin of greater amusement spread on Boisa Pah's lips. Quinne silently nodded his acceptance.

Toohmah studied them a moment, feeling that chill of uncertainty once more. He edged it away. These were no more cautious or reckless than those he had ridden with when he was a young man.

"A few last words," Toohmah said. "I must repeat, I may not kill nor take a scalp on our journey—"

"Your vision." Boisa Pah's voice was steeped in sarcasm. "You have told us this already, old man."

"—and until we cross the Red River"—Toohmah ignored the tall one's comment—"I will lead you. In the land of the *Tejanos,* you may ride where you please. Until then, you follow me without question."

He paused, his gaze moving over the three young faces. Chana's piglike eyes narrowed, and Boisa Pah's mouth uplifted at one corner. Even Quinne's bright eyes blinked.

They understood, he was certain of that. But they did not fully accept it. That was to be expected. Youth was always eager to find ways to slip unnoticed beneath the watchful eyes of the old. He would be hard pressed to keep a tight rein on these three. Once across the river, they would be on their own. Then, he would only help if asked.

"It is time to go," Toohmah said. "Walk on the feet of hunters, and let your tongues sleep until the horses are under us."

Cloaked by the night, Toohmah crouched alone beside the trunk of a wind-snarled sweetgum tree. The leafless branches overhead did nothing to shelter him from the constantly falling rain. Despite his disgust for the white man's clothes he wore, the hat of the *Tejano* cowherders shielded his eyes from the downpour, allowing him clear vision to study the corral before him.

He smiled. An inward excitement coursed through him, bringing alive sensations he had thought were long dead. Lovingly, his gaze caressed the forty head of horses held within the circle of wooden fence. Once he measured his wealth in one hundred fifty horses and thirty mules. Now he ached to sit astride the back of but one of these rain-sleeked mounts.

His attention returned to the two soldiers standing guard on the corral. The cold misery of the night made them careless.

Normally, the guards continually circled the corral, eyes and ears watching the night while they walked side by side.

Tonight, the rain and its chill dulled their caution as water rusts a keenly sharpened blade. A hundred paces from Toohmah's position, they had constructed a makeshift lean-to from tree branches and a piece of canvas. Under this, they built a fire and cooked coffee in a smoke-blackened pot. While one man circled the horses, the other sat beside the fire warming himself. After five circuits of the corral, the soldiers exchanged places.

Toohmah imagined one of the reservation officers coming upon the two. Both would be punished for their behavior. But no officer would be out on such a night, nor at this late hour. The guards realized that, thus found the courage to flaunt the authority of their superiors.

That knowledge, and the fact that there had been no raids on the horses for over five years, was their weakness. A weakness Toohmah hoped to use to his advantage.

The sound of sloshing mud came from behind the old brave. He glanced over a shoulder. Shadows moved within the night's blackness. The sound was too soft for the soldiers or the ears of any White to hear over the rain. Toohmah allowed an overly held breath to escape from between his teeth.

The shadows took form—three crouching men, backs bent by the saddles they carried.

Toohmah listened to their movement. Each footstep sounded distinct to his ears. Once even a squaw of the People moved through the night silently. These reservation-bred *Nermernuh* sounded like stampeding buffalo.

Together the three came to the sweetgum and sank to the ground. Quinne scooted beside Toohmah. "It went quietly. Boisa Pah took the single guard from behind with a rock."

Toohmah saw the tall one grin widely. He nodded his approval of the youth's action.

"It took but a few minutes to pry the lock from the tack room door," Quinne explained. "We did as you said . . . four *Mejano*-style saddles and bridles, plus rope halters and shanks for four more mounts."

"This will not be as simple as the tack room." Toohmah pointed to the corral and briefly outlined his plan. When he finished, Boisa Pah reluctantly surrendered the bottle of whiskey. The old brave eyed Boisa Pah and Chana. "Move quietly. I could hear you coming for a quarter of a mile."

"The guard by the tack room did not hear me, old man," Boisa Pah said with pride. "This one will not either."

Chana grunted his support of his older companion, then the two slipped back into the night to circle behind the corral and wait.

Toohmah watched a few moments, hoping their success at the tack room would not lessen their caution. Timing was essential to his scheme. Both guards must be taken at the same moment. A cry, a warning shot would have every soldier in the reservation garrison down on their backs in a matter of minutes.

"Wait until the soldiers exchange places again before moving." Toohmah looked at Quinne. "And remember, move quietly. One small sound and they will be alerted."

"I shall move like a feather in the air," Quinne said, pulling his hunting knife from its sheath.

Without another word, Toohmah, whiskey bottle in one hand, moved away from the tree into the darkness. Carefully, he skirted the semicircle of light radiating from the campfire. He positioned himself so that he gazed directly into the lean-to, then crouched in the open, hidden only by the night's blackness.

The soldier circling the corral walked past, his head low against his chest to avoid the downpour. Toohmah caught his breath. His heart thudded heavily in his ears. The guard never glanced in Toohmah's direction. The old man smiled; age did not diminish pride.

Within minutes the two guards changed places. As the second soldier began his circuit around the fence, Toohmah saw Quinne's dark form slip from behind the sweetgum and shoot quickly into the shadow cast by the lean-to. The soldier sheltered by the canvas sat on his haunches sipping a fresh cup of coffee. Quinne's movement went unnoticed.

Now if Boisa Pah and Chana were in their positions.

Taking a deep breath, Toohmah stood. He pulled his hat lower to his face and tucked his chin against his chest. Singing to himself, he staggered forward in a perfect mimicry of a drunken brave. He forced himself to walk with a mock, disoriented slowness into the campfire's light.

The guard beneath the lean-to dropped his coffee, scurried from the shelter, and lifted his rifle. "Halt! Identify yourself!"

Toohmah looked up as though startled by the soldier's presence. Then he grinned a broad, silly grin. Waving the bottle before him, he called a greeting to the guard in his own tongue.

The soldier's stance relaxed, the muzzle of the carbine drooping. "You drunken bastard! Go home. You've no business out on a night like this. I could have shot you. I should shoot you. One less stinking Indian to worry about."

Toohmah continued forward, maintaining his charade. He ignored the soldier's words, his attention on Quinne, who crept behind the guard.

The knife blade flashed silver in the campfire's light when the young brave's arm rose and fell. The guard collapsed with a grunt as the knife pommel smacked solidly into the back of his skull.

"Quickly!" Toohmah motioned to the son of his sister's daughter.

They took the carbine and stripped the unconscious soldier of his spare cartridges. Dragging the man beneath the lean-to, they propped him upright as though he sat warming himself. While Quinne returned to the shadows to await Boisa Pah and Chana, Toohmah took cooled ash from the fire and coated the palm of his right hand. He pressed it against the soldier's forehead, leaving the print of a black hand. The first coup of the ride had been taken.

The horses within the corral stirred. Toohmah looked up to see Boisa Pah and Chana climbing over the fence. The two young men smiled widely. Chana hefted a soldier's carbine.

"There was no need to worry, old man," Boisa Pah whispered when he reached Toohmah's side. "The guard never knew we waited for him."

"There will be time for boasting later," the older man answered. "We still have a long night's ride ahead. Chana, Quinne, get the saddles."

Boisa Pah's grin did not diminish. His chest swelled while he surveyed the campfire. Abruptly, a puzzled expression darkened his angular face. "This one lives!"

Before Toohmah could answer, Boisa Pah dropped beside the unconscious man, jerked back his head, and ran his knife across the soldier's exposed throat. A dark line, like a second mouth, opened; blood flowed like a river.

"Now there are two soldiers who will never plague our people again." Boisa Pah stood, chest expanding again as he held out his blade to let the rain wash it clean.

"You killed the other guard?" Toohmah stared at the young man, uncertain he saw and heard correctly.

"I killed them both, old man," Boisa Pah said proudly. "They shall never wake to warn the other soldiers now."

A cold shiver slid along Toohmah's spine. He sought words, but they refused to form.

"Your vision remains intact, old man." Boisa Pah stared at him defiantly. "You have not killed. It is I, Boisa Pah, son of Pihume, who has rid the world of two Whites this night!"

Toohmah's gaze shifted back to the dead soldier. His life's blood pooled around his head in a dark circle on the ground. Dead men were nothing new to him. Had not his own blade eviscerated his enemies to watch them scream in agony? Then why did this one soldier trouble him so? Boisa Pah was correct. He had not killed.

"Uncle," Quinne called to him. The youth stood by the corral's gate. "The horses are ours. Now we can ride!"

Like a man coming out of a dream, Toohmah stepped toward the corral. Ten minutes later, astride a horse, leading another behind him, he rode northward with his three young companions. Toohmah grinned into the face of the night. They would lay a false trail for the soldiers. Several eyes would see them riding, eyes mated to waggling tongues that would be only too willing to sell information to the Whites.

While the soldiers searched the north country for them, they would ride east and follow the Cache River south to the Texas border.

CHAPTER 4

December 19, 1903

The mechanical belching of a horseless carriage dragged Jess Younkin from the black well of sleep. He gathered a quilt about his shoulders to ward off the winter's cold as he sat up. Blinking against the morning light, his eyes focused on a hand-painted sign on the wall opposite the cot, a miniature of the one hung above the Main Street entrance—YOUNKIN AND POTTER LIVERY STABLE, HAAS, TEXAS.

Younkin groaned, in part to answer his head's throbbing and in part with the realization that he had passed out in the stable's tack room last night. He would not escape Mary Ellen's sharp tongue today. His daughter-in-law possessed an unrelenting determination to change habits ingrained by Younkin's sixty years of living. She could not comprehend an old man's occasional need for the companionship of a bottle of bourbon rather than the snug comfort of a room in his son's home.

The rhythmic chug-a-chug outside emphasized the merciless throbbing of Younkin's hangover-swollen head. He rose from the cot to edge aside a dusty curtain that covered the room's single window. Outside, Dixon Milan, owner of the town's feed and seed store, maneuvered a shiny red-and-black Oldsmobile down Haas's Main Street. Milan's was the tenth such contraption in the small West Texas town. Younkin shook his head as dust clouds swirled behind the "progress" promised by the new century. His nose wrinkled at the oily smell of imagined fumes from the noisy engine.

"Jess?" Abe Potter's voice came from the tack room's door, followed by the heavy rap of knuckles on wood. "You up yet?"

Younkin grunted a noncommittal reply. The door opened and Abe entered, bundled in a black, woolen coat. He carried a bucket of steaming water. "Had this left from the hot mash I made for Parker's mare. Thought you might use it to clean up."

With a nod that renewed his head's pounding, Younkin watched his friend and business partner fill a washbasin set atop a table beside a desk on one side of the room. Time had transformed Abe's hair to a thick, white fleece and carved deep lines into his ebony face. The black man's hands trembled while he poured the water, though not a drop spilled. A task Younkin doubted he could duplicate. He sighed. "You're getting old, Abe."

"I know my age." Abe moved to a potbelly stove and removed the cold ashes. "Not like some folks, who stay out till all hours drinking like they still have wild oats to sow . . ."

Or memories to bury. Younkin let the comment pass as he walked to the basin.

". . . A man with a grandson should know better," Abe continued while Younkin opened the table's drawer and extracted a shaving mug and razor. "A man should—"

"A man should know when to keep his mouth shut"—Younkin thumbed open the razor—"or a man might find his black throat cut."

Abe shrugged off the mock threat and stuffed several lumps of coal into the stove. He struck a match and held it to the kindling beneath. "Quicker and easier than a man drinking himself to death."

During the thirty-five years Younkin had known the black, Abe had never allowed him the last word. For the past eight years, since they opened the stable, Abe had grown worse, like an old woman who delighted in worrying herself sick over anything and everything. Abe had been one hell of a soldier and deputy, and a man could not ask for a better friend, but as a business partner . . .

Drinking myself to death. Younkin snorted as he turned to a mirror above the table. Bloodshot eyes stared at him from beneath puffy lids. Gully-deep wrinkles lined the face surrounding those eyes. A thick shock of hair, white as Abe's, stood rumpled atop his head. Time and the Texas sun had weathered his flesh as it molded the harsh land of the High Plains.

Younkin splashed water on his face, then whipped a lather in the mug and brushed it over cheeks and chin. He grimaced while he scraped away the stubble from his face with a dull razor. It was a far cry from the steaming towels and brisk astringents that accompanied the free shaves Ben Simpson had given him at the barbershop when Younkin was Haas's sheriff.

He winced. A drop of blood welled from a nick on his neck. Younkin glanced at Abe's reflection in the mirror. His friend stood warming his hands over the stove. He had not noticed.

Too much whiskey, Younkin admitted to himself. But he was not drinking himself to death. And he was not a drunk. The bourbon made things easier. He could think without years of memories crowding his mind. He slept without dreaming.

When he had served as Haas's sheriff, he had not needed the bourbon. *I shouldn't have retired,* he lied to himself. The mayor and town council had forced him to lay aside his badge. "New blood"—he remembered their words—"a younger man who grasps the changes the country's going through."

First, they brought Charlie Blickle from Dallas. When he moved on to El Paso, the town had elected Younkin's son Tom to fill the office his father had held for ten years.

Younkin felt a mixture of pride and jealousy. Tom was a good man who filled his father's shoes in a way most men only dream of. However, Younkin had not been ready to discard those shoes. He was not cut out to be a livery stable proprietor, relegated to grooming other men's horses, mucking manure from stalls and spreading lime over urine-soaked floors. Other than providing a living, a poor one at that, the stable offered nothing for him.

Should have tried ranching. He drowned the thought as he

bent and washed the remaining soap from his face. His one attempt at working cattle had left him with little more than the shirt on his back. After three years of trying to make a go of it in East Texas, Clara had been only too glad for him to sign on with the Rangers. A lawman's pay had not been much, but it kept a roof over their heads and food on the table. The Rangers eventually led him to the sheriff's office in Haas.

Clara. An aching hollowness filled Younkin's chest when the image of the dark-haired girl he had married in Austin twenty-eight years ago flickered in his mind. Nineteen years and a son they had shared before she died. Bed sickness, Doc Shaw had pronounced, that nebulous term encompassing feminine illness. Clara's death cut the ground out from under him. The world lost its solid feel.

"Jess, we need to talk." Abe's voice, hesitant, intruded into Younkin's memories. "We've got to do something about the bills that have been piling up, not to mention the bank note we owe on the stable."

Younkin nodded, pulled a change of clothes from beneath the cot, and dressed. He had ignored the bills with a childlike faith that he would awake one morning and they would be gone. They had not vanished. Their total climbed toward two hundred dollars. It might as well have been a thousand. The partnership's total capital of a hundred dollars lay stuffed in a cigar box tucked away in a compartment of the tack room's battered rolltop desk. That money was needed to get the stable through the winter.

"What about Mendoza's mules?" Younkin asked. A broad grin spread across Abe's dark face. He had first mentioned the mules a month ago. Younkin had paid no attention to the idea then.

"I think we can buy them for two a head. Mendoza wants to get shut of them. We can drive them into the New Mexico Territory. Loggers are paying ten to twenty a head for good mules." Abe rubbed his hands over the fire.

"Are they harness broke?" Younkin did not relish the prospect of driving fifty mules across the border, but it offered a way from under their debts.

"All broke to the harness. Old man Mendoza intended to sell them as plow animals," Abe answered. "Now that the old man's dead, young Juan wants to sell out quickly, so he and his family can move back to Mexico."

Younkin's sixty years stretched the thought of a trail drive further than it once would have been. Still, it had to be done. "Set things up with Juan. I'll talk with the bank and Milan at the seed and feed. If they understand what we have in mind, maybe they'll stay off our back for another month or so."

"Juan comes in for supplies every Saturday. I'll talk with him today." Abe pulled a pair of leather gloves from a coat pocket and tugged them on his hands. He left the tack room whistling a tune to which Younkin had forgotten the words.

Moving to the desk, Younkin poured himself a shot from a bourbon bottle hidden at the back of the bottom drawer. The whiskey rolled into his stomach hot and raw. Protection from the cold, he told himself, hoping the alcohol would ease the debts from his mind.

Younkin slipped into a fleece-lined coat he took from a wall peg and pushed the collar high about his neck. Pulling a wide-brimmed hat low to his face, he stepped outside. The north wind whistled across the Texas High Plains and into the open stable. Fine dust permeated the air, invading his nostrils. Younkin sneezed, then clamped his teeth together to keep them from chattering as the cold knifed through the layers of his clothing to settle in his joints.

He tried to ignore the arthritic throb in his hands. It persisted. Younkin shook his head. Not even Christmas and the wind held the viciousness of a January blue norther. The winter would be long and cold. The prospect of driving mules into New Mexico seemed more dismal than it had moments ago. Herding fifty head of stock over open trail was no place for a man when a blizzard struck. The wind and cold could freeze flesh on bone, then rip it away.

Younkin walked to the open double doors at the front of the stable. The sky overhead was cloudless; the morning sun bright and harsh. Dust and sand in the air tinted the horizon a light red. Younkin saw no hint of a storm front pushing in from the north laden with snow or, worse, ice.

He surveyed Main Street. Wagons and buckboards lined the wide unpaved avenue. Farmers and ranchers braved the bone-chilling cold to make their weekly trips into town for supplies and reassurance that other human beings populated this flat, desolate country.

Younkin turned to the interior of the lofty stable. Two young boys shot through the door and darted past him. They collapsed atop hay piled in front of a stall, grinning widely at one another, then laughing. Their breath came from their mouths in steamy mists that were whipped away by the wind.

Sternly he stared at the pair in an attempt to disguise the warm pride that suffused him while he eyed his grandson. At seven, Jimmy's long, lanky form hinted of a height that would outstrip his grandfather's six feet when the boy reached manhood. Jimmy's face sobered while he brushed a tossled mop of black hair from his forehead. The child's eyes were as coal-black as those of his grandmother. Even with his somber expression, those eyes sparkled with an impish light Clara's eyes had held. Clara still lived in a grandson she had never seen. The warmth swelled to fill Younkin. At times Jimmy made age and its infirmities seem worth the effort of living, perhaps the only thing.

"What have you young ones been into?" Younkin's voice lacked the firmness he wanted to convey.

"Nothing. Just playing." Jimmy glanced at Harlan Reamy, his redheaded companion. The hint of a grin formed on Jimmy's lips, then he suppressed it.

Younkin doubtfully shook his head. Jimmy and Haas's newspaper editor's son had all the spirit and life of two colts that just had discovered the power of their long, spindly legs. Mischief walked hand in hand with the pair.

For a moment, Younkin considered pursuing what prank they had managed to escape from, then let the matter pass. "You two run along. There's work to be done and no time for playing. Now, if you've a mind to help with the stalls, I'd appreciate the extra hands."

Jimmy looked at the pitchfork and muck basket set beside the hay. Dubiously, he turned back to his grandfather. "Papaw, Harlan doesn't believe you were a Texas Ranger."

Jimmy's freckle-faced companion scrutinized Younkin like a stockman examining the conformation of a horse, then moved his head from side to side. "Too old for a Ranger, and I ain't never seen him carry no gun, except maybe a shotgun for rabbits."

Younkin smiled. "I was a mite younger when I rode with the Rangers."

"He killed Yankees in the Civil War and was an Indian scout too." Jimmy's chest swelled with pride. "Papaw was sheriff here before my pa."

"Ever see John Wesley Hardin?" Harlan asked doubtfully.

"Once, down San Angelo ways," Younkin answered. "I didn't pay him no nevermind. He wasn't breaking the law, and there was no need to go about stirring up trouble."

"You never saw him shoot it out with anybody?" There was disappointment in Harlan's voice.

"No, but I saw Doc Holliday and a man draw down on each other in Dallas." Younkin noted the boys' eyes brighten. "They were in a saloon. Stood about twenty feet apart. Each fired three times. Missed with every shot."

"You mean Doc Holliday didn't kill the man?" Jimmy's brow furrowed. Harlan shook his head. "Don't believe it."

"Cartridges used to be filled with black powder. They weren't as accurate as the store-bought cartridges now," Younkin explained. "A man was never sure if he had a good load or not."

"What about the Comanches?" Jimmy beamed at his grandfather. "Tell Harlan about them."

Years crept into Younkin's mind, half-forgotten incidents alive and vivid. "What do you want to know about the Comanche?"

"Better stop your reminiscing." Abe walked into the stable. "Miss Mary Ellen's coming this way. She looks like she's got a burr under her blanket."

Younkin glanced at the boys. They nodded in unison before he could ask Jimmy if his mother was looking for him.

"We're hiding from Miss Overcash." Jimmy's eyes lowered. "We played hooky Wednesday. She's wanting us to make it up today. Must've told Ma we didn't show up at school."

"Schooling's good, but not on Saturday." Younkin pointed to a ladder that rose to the stable's hayloft. "Hide and keep quiet. I'll cover for you with your ma."

The two boys scampered into the loft and dropped behind a pile of hay an instant before Younkin's daughter-in-law appeared in the doorway. "Where are they, Jess?"

Younkin smiled politely at the deceptively small woman. Mary Ellen had a mind of her own and the determination to back it up. "Morning, Mary Ellen. You look as pretty as a fashion plate today."

"Sweet talk won't help, Jess Younkin." The raven-haired woman's hands went to her hips. "Tom thought he saw Jimmy and the Reamy boy run in here."

"Haven't seen Jimmy since yesterday afternoon." Younkin scratched at his chin and shook his head. "The boy in trouble again?"

Ignoring the question, Mary Ellen stalked up and down the stable to give the stalls a cursory examination. "If I find them, I'll tan their backsides."

"Haven't seen Jim all morning," Younkin repeated.

The young woman's right eyebrow arched in reproach. "Guess you might be telling the truth, or else you wouldn't have let me look in here." She looked at Younkin, then Abe. "If you see those boys, tell them they'd better get to the school before I find them."

"I'll do that, Mary Ellen." Younkin followed his daughter-in-law to the door and watched her walk down the street with short, quick strides.

In front of Barrett's General Store, she stopped and hailed her husband, who walked toward the sheriff's office. Younkin's son lifted his hat, scratched his scalp, and shook his head.

With a wave of her arms, Mary Ellen stormed down the street.

Watching Tom enter his office, Younkin smiled, pleased with his small deception. Mary Ellen was a good woman, none better in the county, but she was straight as a yardstick and too unbending at times.

"She knew the boys were here, listening to your tales." Abe twisted his mouth in disapproval. "If she finds out, she'll be after more than their backsides."

"You worry too much." Younkin motioned to the loft. "Tell the boys to stay put until she cools down. I'll be back in a little while."

"Where you off to?" Abe asked. "There's work to be done around here."

Younkin waved his friend away, knowing Abe could handle the stalls alone for one morning. Yanking his collar higher, Younkin started toward the sheriff's office. There was no purpose in postponing the inevitable. He drew a prolonged breath between his teeth, wishing for a shot or two from the bottle in the desk. It would make things easier. No man liked to go begging to his son.

CHAPTER 5

The office was an estranged friend, familiar yet alien. The pine walls, dark knots memorized during endless hours alone within their confines; the worn floors, scarred by years of uncaring boots and heavy spurs; fogged windows, smudged in halfhearted attempts to wipe away caked dust; coughs and groans from ranch hands, recovering from lost battles with whiskey bottles, in four cells beyond the door at the back of the office: the effluvium of bitter, boiled coffee, stale tobacco, and gun oil—over the years, each had leeched away something vital that had been Jess Younkin, then cast him aside. The office taunted him, refusing to return what it had taken or offer the secure comfort it once had given free.

"Morning, Pa." Tom sat beside a square-built cast-iron stove with his deputies. Henry Wells and Frank Galvin acknowledged Younkin's entrance with a nod. "Hank was saying he expected trouble tonight."

Drawn by the aroma of burning mesquite wood, Younkin moved to the stove and glanced at Wells, a short, stocky man who sported a drooping moustache. He wore threadbare khaki trousers tucked into the tops of battered, round-toed boots. A frayed white shirt poked out around the collar of a faded-brown, woolen coat. Pushed back from Wells's forehead was a sweat-stained hat that had lost any trace of crease or roll.

Wells would have been a hard-case occupant of the jail if Tom had not taken him under his wing and given him a job. While the man could never be called a quick thinker, Wells was reliable and loyal. He would follow Tom into hell itself if he were asked.

"It's the Grant brothers." Wells displayed the gaps of two missing lower teeth when he spoke. "Both of them act like studs that's got the scent of a horsing mare when they get around that new gal at Pilgrim's Saloon."

"Get a couple of beers in them, and they'll be at one another like the Great John L. and Gentleman Jim," Frank Galvin added. "Then Will Martin and his hands will get in on it."

Galvin was the complete opposite of Wells: lean, tall, clean shaven, and immaculately dressed. From his black derby to his spit-polished spats, Galvin looked like a dandy who had just stepped out of a *Saturday Evening Post* illustration. The appearance was deceptive. Galvin could take care of himself, as more than one cowhand had discovered when they decided to take a poke at the fancy-dressing deputy.

"Last time the Grants got into it, two men ended up with cracked ribs and another busted a hand." Tom rose and walked to a window. "Don't look forward to dealing with them. Too cold for nonsense."

"Not much to worry over." Younkin patted his coat pockets and realized he had left his pipe in the tack room. Galvin offered him a pack of ready-rolled cigarettes. Younkin took one and lit it from the stove. It lacked the taste of a pipe. "We used to have shootings every Saturday night. If men—"

"The old days . . ." Sarcasm seeped in Wells's voice as he slipped a tobacco twist from a pocket and bit off a chew. ". . . if a man listened to you, he'd believe Jesse James, the Dalton boys, and William Bonney all lived here in Haas."

"Never said those types rode this way." Younkin ignored Galvin's amused chuckle. "Though once I ran Richard Brinsley Sheridan Clark out of town."

"Who's he? A character out of a dime novel?" Galvin winked at the other deputy.

Wells spit a stream of tobacco juice into a tin can beside his chair. "He rode with Butch Cassidy till he shot his horse drawing down on Jess. Then he walked with Butch Cassidy."

The two deputies laughed, pleased by their wit. Younkin

shook his head sadly. Neither had ever heard of Dick Clark, one of Tombstone's most infamous gamblers.

"I like the story about the time Jess and Abe were surrounded by a hundred Apaches on the warpath," Galvin continued. "They were out of ammunition when the Indians charged."

"What happened then, old man?" Wells's eyes were bright with mirth.

"Never were any Apache in this part of Texas. Quanah Parker and his—" Younkin tried to explain.

"Hell, Hank," Galvin's voice rose to drown out Younkin, "Jess and Abe were killed, of course."

The two young men bellowed with laughter. Younkin stood mutely staring with bewilderment, unsure how or why he had become the butt of their jokes.

"That'll be enough." Tom sat behind his desk, a reprimanding glare shifting between the deputies. "Haven't you got better things to do?"

Wells rose to check the cells and Galvin picked up a newspaper from the floor. Tom glanced at his father, then turned his attention to a stack of papers on the desk. A rush of embarrassed heat mingled with Younkin's confusion. Shame tightened his chest. Did his son have to defend him against the verbal barbs of younger men? Had it come to that?

Younkin studied his son. Except for a wider mouth and shorter nose he had inherited from his mother, Tom could have been his father at twenty-seven. The height, the build, the hair, the intense look, all had once belonged to a younger Jess Younkin.

Tom's gaze rose to his father again. He smiled, a smile that increased the cramping in his father's chest. It was a reassuring smile an adult used to comfort a child. Had the years convoluted to leave the child father to the father?

Quietly, Younkin sank into a chair beside his son's desk. Attempting to bypass his pride, he mentally groped for the phrasing with which to begin.

"Pa," Tom leaned back in his chair, "can I help you with something?"

His throat desiccate and scratchy, Younkin swallowed. His eyes shifted to the floor. "Money problems."

"Again?" Reproach edged into Tom's tone.

Younkin's chest heaved, then he explained the pressing debts, Abe's scheme to buy Mendoza's mules and sell them to New Mexican loggers. "A hundred and fifty would be nice, but we could make do with a hundred."

"A hundred . . ." The words came as a question spoken aloud while Tom pondered the proposal. Then silence. Finally, he said, "I'll see if I can manage it. Just don't tell Mary Ellen. I don't believe she would—"

"Now here's something!" Galvin held up the paper he had been reading to interrupt Tom's cautious warning. "Someone finally built a machine that can fly!"

Galvin tossed a copy of *The Dallas Morning News* to Tom, who spread it atop the desk. Younkin leaned close to read a page-three article datelined Norfolk, Virginia, December 18:

FLYING MACHINE A SUCCESS

Wilbur and Orville Wright Fly Their
Craft in Face of Stiff Breeze

No Balloon Attachment

A successful trial trip of a flying machine was made yesterday near Kitty Hawk, N.C., by Wilbur and Orville Wright of Dayton, Ohio. The machine flew for three miles in the face of wind blowing at a registered velocity of twenty-one miles an hour, and then gracefully descended to the earth at the spot selected by the man in the navigator's car as a suitable landing place. The machine has no balloon attachment, but gets its force from propellers worked by a small engine.

A "Special to The News" from Dayton, Ohio, reported that the machine was supported by "aerocurves," or wings, forty feet long, traveled at thirty-one miles an hour, and was driven by an engine that "develops sixteen break-horsepower." The craft's longest flight had been fifty-seven seconds.

Wishing an illustration accompanied the article, Younkin tried to envision such a machine. He could not. The image of Dixon Milan's horseless carriage with long, flapping bird wings was ridiculous.

"Never thought anyone would do it." Tom emphasized his amazement with a sharp whistle, then started reading aloud a short article about Chicago vying with New York for the Democratic National Convention next year.

"What's the matter, Jess?" Galvin grinned at Younkin while he unfolded the weekly edition of the Haas *Gazette*. "Look like you felt someone walking on your grave."

"Men actually flying in the air." Younkin cocked his head to one side. What possible use was there to it? Dixon Milan claimed horseless carriages would make it unnecessary for a man to ride a horse or even walk one day. He found that hard to accept. All such contraptions did was stir up dust, stink, and scare livestock. The world had no use for them. Maybe those eastern Yankees did, but they had no purpose in West Texas.

"Here's something more in your line, old man." Galvin pointed to an article in the *Gazette*. "Says here some old Indian and three young bucks killed two soldiers at Fort Sill in Oklahoma, then escaped the reservation. One soldier was found with a handprint of ash on his forehead."

"A handprint?" Younkin shoved from his chair and walked to the deputy, leaning over his shoulder. Forgotten sensations stirred as Younkin scanned the recount of the murders.

"What's this about Indians on the warpath?" Wells reentered the office.

"Some of Jess's old Comanche friends killed a couple of soldiers at Fort Sill," Galvin answered as Younkin read the list of escapees' names: Quinne, Chana, Boisa Pah, and Toohmah.

"Black Hand!" Younkin's eyes widened. "The bastard's still alive."

"Damn if you ain't right, Frank." Wells elbowed his companion's ribs. "It *is* one of the old man's buddies!"

Younkin ignored the two, finishing the article. "Fools!"

"What's the matter?" Tom glanced up.

"Says the Army is searching for Black Hand and the other three north of Fort Sill. Black Hand's Comanche. He'd never ride north, except to lay a false trail. He'd move south into Texas, then west. The High Plains, this whole area, was where he roamed with Quanah Parker's band."

"Don't see where it concerns you." Wells spit into the tin can. "Reckon it's the Army's trouble."

"Besides, the Army thinks they're headed for the Canadian border." Galvin winked at Wells. "You're not telling us you know better than the United States Army, are you, Jess?"

"The Army learns a thing one day and forgets it the next." Younkin began to explain who Black Hand was, how he had terrorized the early Texas frontier. The words and memories jumbled together incoherently. There were too many of them to place in clear, concise sentences. In a stammer, Younkin stopped.

Wells and Galvin grinned widely. Their expressions were worse than words. They did not believe him. He was no more than a babbling, senile old fool to them. How could they understand? The Comanche had been banished from the High Plains before they had been a gleam in their fathers' eyes.

Tom's head turned to his father. His chest heaved as though trying to relieve itself of an unwanted burden. "I agree with Frank and Henry, Pa. It's Army business. It doesn't concern us."

"And I tell you, Black Hand is heading this way. This land was his home. Are you going to sit on your backside and let him ride up to your doorstep? He's already killed two men!" Incredulously, Younkin stared at his son. "You're a lawman. It's your job to do what you can. You should telegraph Fort Sill and tell them they're wrong."

"Pa, times have changed. My jurisdiction ends at the county line." Younkin sensed an underlying irritation within his son. "Indians are government business. The Army will handle the situation in their own way. They don't want a small-town sheriff butting in."

Before Younkin could reply, the office door flew open. Mary Ellen stood at the threshold, hands mounted firmly on her hips. Her gaze homed in on her father-in-law. Younkin swallowed his greeting, realizing a word from him would ignite the anger the woman barely held in rein.

Mary Ellen's head jerked to her husband. "Thomas Ward Younkin, I want to speak to you—in private!"

Without hesitation, Tom rose and followed his wife outside. The door closed behind them. Younkin watched the two through the dust-and-moisture-smeared window. He could not hear above the constant howl of the wind, but Mary Ellen's face was no more than an inch from Tom's, and her lips never stopped moving. Now and then, her arm would fly in the air, and she jabbed a finger toward the office.

"Wheeeew!" Wells whistled. "That's one man whose shoes I wouldn't be in right now for a hundred greenbacks."

Galvin chuckled. "There's not a man in Haas who'd face Mary Ellen when she's on a tear."

With a final angry glance to the window, Mary Ellen swung from her husband and walked away in those same short, quick, impatient strides Younkin had seen earlier. The office door opened and Tom poked his head inside.

"Pa, we need to talk." It was the command of an adult summoning a wayward child.

Younkin felt Wells's and Galvin's eyes follow him outside. Tom yanked the door closed behind his father. He waited for a wagon to pass on the street before he turned to his father.

"Damn it, Pa, what's got into you?" Anger flushed Tom's cheeks. "Mary Ellen found Jim and Harlan Reamy hiding in the stable. They said you knew they were running away from Miss Overcash."

"It's Saturday. A schoolhouse is no place for boys on Saturday," Younkin replied. "Don't see why you're—"

Tom did not allow his father to finish. "Fishing Wilson's tank on Wednesday wasn't where Jim was supposed to be either. Seems Jim picked that idea up from you."

"You can't blame me for—" Younkin stopped. He recalled telling his grandson about how he had played hooky as a boy in East Texas.

"You didn't do it on purpose. But part of the responsibility for the tricks Jim's been pulling lately is yours. Mary Ellen and I believe all the stories you've been telling him about the old days are putting notions into his head." Tom paused for a breath. "Pa, it's not the way it used to be. It's the twentieth century. You read it in the newspaper today. Men are flying. No telling what will come next. That's the world I'm preparing Jim for."

"What I *was* is all I've got." Younkin turned from his son in an attempt to conceal his bruised pride. "There's no harm in telling my own grandson how this country used to be."

"There is if it gives him the wrong ideas. Can't you see? There aren't any more Comanche, no more gunmen running wild. When you came to Haas, there were less than a hundred people here. Now, there's over fifteen hundred. We're almost a city." Tom's chest heaved heavily. "Pa, I love you, and I've got no want to hurt you . . . but unless you quit filling Jim's head with wild dreams about times that don't exist anymore . . . well . . . Mary Ellen and I think it would be best to keep the boy away from you."

Younkin's head snapped around. He stared at his son, uncertain he had heard correctly. Tom's expression left no doubt of his son's sincerity. "Tom, I . . . I . . ." He could not work the words over the lump lodged in his throat. They wanted to take Jim away from him. They would rob him of the only thing that seemed to matter to him anymore.

"And your drinking, Pa. You've got to stop staying out all night like a common drunk. You've got to help set a good example for Jim." Tom's gaze held on his father. "There's no ands, ifs, or buts about it, Pa. Mary Ellen and I know what's best for the boy. You've got to help us give it to him, not stand in the way."

Younkin had not been prepared for this, never suspected it. Tom and his family were all that remained to him. Had he lost their love along with everything else he held dear? Without them, without Jim, there would be nothing. He nodded, his voice coming soft and subdued. "You're right. The old days are dead. You and Mary Ellen won't have to worry about me giving Jim wild notions anymore. I'll do whatever you want."

Younkin turned and started back to the stable, feeling like a cowed dog with its tail between its legs. "Pa," Tom called, but Younkin kept walking. He heard the office door open and close behind him.

Tom was right, he told himself. Times had changed. Haas was no longer a small supply town for ranchers. It had grown to a place where people came to raise their families. The gunmen, the cattle drives, the gamblers, the Comanche, all belonged to the past.

Younkin's gaze drifted along Main Street. Time left him estranged from the town and its residents. When he first rode the High Plains, Haas had not existed, just the Comanche and the buffalo. Dead and gone. A memory locked in the mind of an old man.

The Comanche; the *Gazette* article flashed to mind. *Black Hand.* All of the past was not dead. Remnants, ugly and vicious, of the past remained. Remnants that could still kill.

Younkin pivoted on the balls of his feet and strode toward the telegraph office. If Tom would not do something about Black Hand, he would.

CHAPTER 6

December 25, 1903

Toohmah halted the bay he rode at the edge of a steep bank that dropped ten feet to meet a dark band of water. The prospect of fording the river the Whites call the Trinity at night and in the biting cold left the old Comanche uneasy.

Only thirty feet separated him from the opposite bank. That the water flowed far below the crest of its bank told him winter rains had yet to swell the river to its full might. However, when he studied the Trinity in a side glance, the moon did not provide enough light to discern the water's features. He could not judge the current or the depth.

"Remove your clothes and hold them high above your heads when you cross." Toohmah could delay no longer and waste the night's cloak that concealed their movements.

"We ride naked into the water?" Boisa Pah's voice conveyed the scowl the darkness hid from Toohmah's eyes. "Old man, the air itself is freezing about us."

"More the reason for dry clothing when we reach the opposite bank." Swinging from the gelding, Toohmah quickly stripped away the white man's clothing he wore.

The slight breeze that stirred the dry vegetation along the bank felt like an icy knife raking against his bare skin. He clamped his teeth together to stop them from rattling in his head. If he displayed no outward signs of discomfort, the others would follow his lead, the pride of youth refusing to be shamed by an old man's strength.

Clothes bundled in his coat, Toohmah remounted the bay.

His bare buttocks drew into taunt balls as they tried to escape contact with the saddle's chilled leather. Beside him, Quinne and Chana slid from their mounts and began to shed their clothing. With a disapproving grunt, Boisa Pah did likewise.

The old *Nermernuh* slowly shook his head. Since their escape from the reservation nine days ago, Boisa Pah had been a constant thorn in his side. With Chana in agreement, the lanky brave sought to exert himself as the leader of the small band. He mocked Toohmah's insistence that they ride at night to avoid the white man's eyes. He laughed at Toohmah's cautiously wide, zigzagging path across North Central Texas, designed to confuse any who might attempt to track them. He complained when the old warrior refused to allow him to hunt with the carbine he had stolen from the soldiers. Instead Toohmah, with bow and arrow, silently downed a farmer's stray mule or a rancher's steer when the band happened upon them. As with all the People who rode this land before them, they gorged themselves on the fresh meat, then traveled on empty bellies until game presented itself again. This, too, Boisa Pah found fault in, bemoaning both overstuffed and hollow stomach.

Toohmah's attention shifted from his companions to the land surrounding them. Rolling plains, spotted by oaks, willows, and sweetgums stripped bare by winter, spread out on all sides. Here and there, he detected the dark forms of evergreen cedars clumped together in thick brakes. Faint pinpricks of light, at least two miles to the south, marked a white man's dwelling. To the north, other lights glowed.

So many. The Whites were like rabbits breeding without the coyote to keep their numbers in check. Farms and ranches sprouted across the prairie like bull thistle after a spring shower.

A shivery lance of horror jabbed within his chest at the memory of what had filled his eyes two nights past. He had sought to ford the Trinity near the White settlement of Dallas. He had topped a rolling rise and stared below in disbelief. When he had last seen the settlement it had been no more than a tiny cluster of crude cabins and tents. In twenty-eight years, it had multiplied a hundredfold. Houses and buildings stood close together like blue ticks on the shoulders of a wolf. Smoke billowed from a thousand chimneys, covering the land with an unnatural haze. Even now the stench clung to his nose.

"Uncle"—Quinne's voice brought the old man from his thoughts—"we are ready."

Drawing naked legs high on the bay's shoulders, Toohmah nudged the horse forward. The gelding balked an instant, then plunged down the embankment, scrambling with its forelegs and sitting back on its haunches. The crisp cracking of thin ice breaking came from under its hooves as they sank into the black water. Again Toohmah's heels nudged the bay. It lunged into the river.

The brave smiled; good fortune remained his. The water rose only to the horse's belly. Breath coming in labored snorts from flared nostrils, the gelding crossed the river, scrambled up the opposite bank, and shook itself. A shower of cold-burning droplets splattered over the Comanche's naked skin. He shivered in spite of himself.

Dropping from the gelding, Toohmah waved the others on, then unraveled his clothing to dress. Defiantly, Boisa Pah reined his black mare down the bank into the freezing river. Quinne, astride a chestnut, followed at his heels. Hesitating at the bank's edge for several heartbeats, Chana finally kicked his mount's flanks and swung his legs to the horse's shoulders.

With a disapproving cluck of his tongue, Toohmah dressed. Chana's life would have been short when the *Nermernuh* ruled the plains. The pig-faced youth lacked a brave's courage.

The splashing and hollow clop of hooves moving up the bank sounded to the old brave as loud as javelinas running through dense underbrush. He glanced around to once more assure himself they were too far from the Whites' houses to be heard.

"Aaiiee!" A startled cry jerked Toohmah's head back to the river. Chana and his mount lay fallen halfway up the embankment. While Boisa Pah and Quinne rode up from the river,

Toohmah scrambled downward on foot to the toppled rider and horse.

His left arm clutched to his chest, Chana kicked clear from his thrashing mount. The horse rolled and pawed the air in an attempt to regain its footing. It never would. Toohmah saw the grotesque, angular bend of its right foreleg, a broken shin.

A bullet would have been quicker, easier, but he dared not risk the noise. Freeing the hunting knife at his waist, the aged brave slid down the bank until he grasped the horse's ear and twisted. For an instant, the injured animal lay motionless. The Comanche's arm lashed out, drawing the blade across the horse's neck to sever the jugular vein.

Before the horse realized what had occurred, Toohmah rolled beside Chana. The animal came to life again. It kicked and snorted with violent energy, sensing that only a few moments remained before its life gushed from its opened neck. A minute, five, Toohmah watched the death throes, feeling a rootless sorrow that separated him from the scene. Eventually, the horse lay motionless, its broad sides no longer heaving.

"My arm, it's broken." Pain permeated Chana's whining voice. He still cradled his left arm.

Without a word, Toohmah helped the younger man to his feet, then wrapped an arm about Chana's wide waist to support him as they half-walked, half-crawled to the top of the bank. Two hundred feet downriver grew a cedar brake. Ordering the three younger men into its cover, the old Comanche slid down the bank to retrieve Chana's dropped clothing. He then scooted to the lifeless horse, freed the saddle's girt, and tugged the saddle from beneath the dead weight.

When he rejoined his companions, Toohmah took what remained of Boisa Pah's whiskey from his saddlebag. He tossed the bottle to Chana and ordered him to drink. While the pig-faced one complied, Toohmah hacked two stout limbs from a cedar and stripped them. Cutting the left arm from the injured man's shirt, he tore it into four long strips.

"You ride like a woman." Boisa Pah glared at his friend with disgust. "We can not afford injuries."

"My horse lost its footing," Chana whined weakly. "It wasn't my fault."

Toohmah paid no heed to the exchange as he squatted at Chana's side. Directing Quinne to firmly hold his companion's shoulder, the brave's hands explored the injured arm and located the fracture. He looked up at Chana. "There will be pain, but the arm must be set. Take a deep breath and release it slowly."

As Chana sucked in, Toohmah lifted his wrist and pulled the arm straight. Chana groaned, his body tensing for a moment, but he did not cry out as the broken bone slipped into place. Quickly, Toohmah used the branches and torn cloth to bind a splint about the arm.

"What now, old man?" Boisa Pah spoke while Toohmah helped Chana stretch out on the ground. "The arm will be useless for weeks."

"Only one arm is needed to rein a horse." Toohmah stood and relocated the distant lights to the south. "We will steal another mount."

"The risk is too great. Even with a fresh horse, he will hinder us." Boisa Pah hovered over his injured companion. "The arm is his problem, not ours."

Chana pushed from the ground with his good arm. "I can ride. The arm causes no pain now."

"With a belly full of whiskey, no one feels pain. What of tomorrow when there is no whiskey?" Boisa Pah turned to Toohmah and Quinne. "Let him find and steal his own horse. We should ride south into the land of the *Mejanos*."

"Leave him?" Quinne's head moved from side to side as though uncertain whether he understood what his companion suggested. "How would he hunt? The Whites will find and kill him."

"A risk we all accepted when we fled the reservation," Boisa Pah replied without hesitation. "Old man, what do you think?"

Toohmah smiled to himself. Boisa Pah never rested in his attempts to assume leadership. "You are right. Chana will hinder us. He should be left on his own."

"Uncle?" Shock filled Quinne's voice. Boisa Pah chuckled, sensing victory.

"No! You can't leave me!" Chana's words came in high-pitched fear.

"Nor will I," Toohmah said. "Nor, do I believe, will Quinne. However, it was agreed that each of us could ride his own way after crossing the Red River. That time is eight days past. Boisa Pah may ride south to Mexico anytime he wishes."

Toohmah felt the tension that suffused the tall, angular brave. Though he could not see Boisa Pah's countenance in the dark, he sensed the anger that clouded his face.

"Will you stay, or ride by yourself?" Quinne asked.

Boisa Pah stiffened. He stood rigid and silent for a long moment, then his shoulders slumped flaccidly. "Stay."

Toohmah looked down at Chana. "Dress and hide yourself among the cedars until we return."

They rode in a wide circle around the ranch house, three shadows that moved among shadows. It was easy. The *Tejanos* no longer feared a Comanche raid on their stock. Why should they? Toohmah realized. The People had not ridden the plains in twenty-eight years. Tonight, at least one rancher would relearn the stealth and cunning by which a Comanche steals horses from beneath the noses of his enemies.

Open and vulnerable, the house sat unprotected except for two barren oaks growing to its south side. Bright lights glared from the house's windows. Inside, men and women moved. Occasionally, their voices lifted in song. Toohmah recognized the tunes as those taught by the reservation Quakers, songs that told of the birth of their god Jesus. For the *Nermernuh* a belief in greater spirits than man was a private matter. Medicine belonged to an individual, not to be shared in song with others.

Of more interest was the large barn situated to the east of the house. Corrals on both sides of the structure lay empty. The barn's closed doors indicated the horses were sheltered within for the night. It would be easier to take fresh mounts from stalls than to have to run them down in the corrals.

Toohmah allowed himself a satisfied smile. Best of all, he saw no dogs around the house. Without the warning barks of watchdogs to announce their approach, they should be able to walk into the barn and quietly lead away the horses without drawing the attention of those celebrating within the house.

Toohmah reined the gelding toward the seclusion of a slight hill that rose behind the barn. Quinne and Boisa Pah followed. Concealed by the rise, he dismounted and tied his reins to a large stone on the ground. In a crouched run, the aged brave topped the hill and squatted there until his two companions joined him.

"We will enter the barn and take all the horses we find." He studied the house and barn a hundred yards beyond their position. Still he saw no dogs. "Move quietly and speak only if needed."

Again in a half-crouch, Toohmah trotted toward the barn with the younger men beside him. The barn's double doors were held closed by a single board. Noiselessly, Quinne lifted it from its niches and pulled a door open enough to admit him. Boisa Pah entered after Quinne, then Toohmah, who pulled the door closed behind him.

For a moment, Toohmah stood motionless, allowing his eyes to accustom themselves to a blackness deeper than the night. The warmth of living things huddled together within a closed space edged back the cold that resided in his joints. He breathed deeply. The mingling aromas of cow, horse, hay, grain, and freshly dropped manure filled his nostrils. They were good, natural smells.

"Four horses and two cows kept for milking." Quinne came to him out of the barn's interior darkness.

"Only the horses," Toohmah answered after discarding the possibility of stealing a cow for meat tomorrow. A cow would hinder their flight.

While Quinne strode to the rearmost stalls, and Boisa Pah disappeared into one near the door, Toohmah slowly examined the barn. To his right stood an empty stall. The dark forms of swollen grain sacks stood within. While a full bag of oats or sweet feed would be too much added weight to carry, half of a sack would be manageable and would provide the horses nourishment dry winter grass could not.

Drawing his knife, the old warrior slashed open the mouth of one burlap bag. He tilted the sack, spilling oats onto the barn's floor. When the bag was half empty, he twisted its top, tied it in a knot, and threw the sack over a shoulder. Satisfied he could carry the weight until they reached their hidden mounts, Toohmah stepped toward the doors.

He froze. Footsteps came from outside.

"Damn, Jake must've left the barn open." A man's voice came from beyond the door. Another answered. "He's had a mite too much Christmas spirit . . . all from a jug."

The barn door swung open. Light from the house flooded into the barn. Quinne, leading a horse in each hand, stood in the middle of the barn, blinded by the unexpected illumination. Two men stepped inside.

"I'll be . . ." The man nearest Toohmah dropped a wooden bucket. Water splashed into the air. "A goddamn horse thief."

The white man's right hand dropped to a revolver holstered on his hip. Simultaneously, Toohmah swung the sack of oats with all his weight behind the blow. The bag slammed into the back of the White's head. The man staggered forward, dazed, gun falling from unsteady fingers.

From the corner of an eye, Toohmah saw an arm shoot out of the darkness, clamp a hand around the other white man's mouth, and wrench him into the blackness of the stall Boisa Pah had entered.

Toohmah yanked his hunting knife free of its sheath. The *nenuhpee* warning echoed in his mind. He pushed through the urge to remain motionless. Raising the knife high, he rushed behind the still-standing man. With all his strength, he swung the knife down in a wide arc. A sharp crack echoed in the barn as the knife's pommel struck squarely against the back of the man's skull.

A low moan quavered over the white man's lips. For a heartbeat, he stood, swaying from side to side. Abruptly, his legs folded under him and he collapsed to lie still on the barn's dirt floor.

Toohmah dropped beside the unconscious man. He pressed an ear to the White's chest. The man's heart still beat; he still breathed. Toohmah had not killed.

Satisfied, the Comanche reached into a pocket to withdraw a charred piece of mesquite wood he now carried. He darkened his right hand with the charcoal and pressed his palm to the man's pale forehead. Coup taken, Toohmah rose and waved Quinne and the horses from the barn.

Boisa Pah stepped from the dark stall. He wiped blood from his hunting knife on a handful of straw. A holster and pistol were draped over one shoulder. When he saw Toohmah, the young brave grinned widely and made a slow slashing motion with the blade in front of his throat. The gesture left no doubt as to how Boisa Pah had disposed of the other white man.

"Brag of your kills later. Get the horse and follow Quinne," Toohmah ordered in a harsh whisper.

Boisa Pah grinned again and ducked back into the stall. Kneeling beside the unconscious man once more, Toohmah stripped away his holster and retrieved the pistol from the ground. Strapping the gun about his waist, he then led the last horse from its stall and followed Boisa Pah from the barn. Only when they reached their waiting mounts did he remember the oats left on the barn's floor.

The whiskey ran thin in Chana's veins; its numbing effects wore off. Toohmah sensed the twinges of reawakening pain in the way Chana shielded the arm. The young brave would slow their progress, as would tonight's raid. The soldiers would soon hear of the white man and his slit throat and come scouring the *Tejanos'* lands in search of them.

"We will ride northwest along the river for a mile, then ride southeast, letting the river's current hide our tracks." Toohmah nudged the bay's flanks with his heels, moving along the bank of the Trinity River toward Dallas.

He did not like wasting time laying a false trail, but it was necessary. Before they finally halted their easterly movement, he would be ever farther from the High Plains in the west. Yet to do less would deliver them into the soldiers' hands.

I did not kill, Toohmah bolstered himself in face of the untimely delays. I hold true to the *nenuhpee*'s words.

CHAPTER 7

January 13, 1904

Jess Younkin peered out the tack room's window. The West Texas weather played like a capricious child easily bored with his toys. That morning a dreary, misting rain had shrouded the town, followed by snow flurries. Haas's streets had been transformed into a mire of slush and mud.

By noon, the low-hanging gray clouds dissipated. The sun reigned, drinking away the excess moisture that had been mistakenly doled out to this ever-thirsty land. Now, the streets appeared as parched as in a summer drought. The wind, dust and sand caught in its invisible hand, tossed sapless, tangled husks of tumbleweeds down Main Street in rolling disarray.

"They should've shot the man who introduced Russian thistle into this land." An undefined sadness moved in Younkin. The plant was alien to this country, introduced in the New Mexico Territory as ground cover to protect the thin topsoil. It had spread like wildfire throughout the Southwest: a thick, leafy weed in summer, a tumbling, wind-tossed skeleton in winter.

"We aren't here to talk about tumbleweeds. We've got a couple hundred dollars in debts to worry about. Our creditors would just as soon close us down and take this stable away as look us in the eye." Abe made no attempt to conceal his impatience. "We promised the bank, the feed and seed, the general store, old man Reasoner—all of them—they'd have their money by the end of the month."

Younkin continued to stare at the wooden buildings that

lined Main Street. When he first arrived in Haas, he used to gaze from the sheriff's office over the open plains. He once read of the great oceans, how their vast expanses ruled the souls of men who went to sea. He had understood the power that molded men to its whim when he searched the miles of endless prairie. Love, hate, joy, sorrow, meant nothing to the land. It demanded acceptance for what it was; change it and the land would eventually kill a man.

Dixon Milan wheeled his horseless carriage home from a day at his store. Its mechanical belching rumbled over the sound of the wind. Younkin turned from the window to escape the heaviness that crowded around him from all sides. He looked at Abe, his friend's stooped, bent shoulders supporting the same invisible weight.

"Damn that man from Lubbock to hell!" Abe repeated the curse Younkin had heard a thousand times in the past three days. "Beat us to them mules by two bits a head. Damn Juan Mendoza!"

"The boy sold cheap and took the best offer. Money is money." Younkin leaned against a tack box, resigned to the fact that they had been outbid on the mules. "Nothing we can do about it."

Abe shook his head in disgust. "You don't look worried. Any ideas where we're going to raise two hundred dollars?"

Younkin did not answer. A cockroach scurried across the floor. He lifted a boot, crushed it beneath his heel, then kicked the mashed body down a crack in the floor.

"What about Tom?" Abe suggested. "Could you ask him?"

"No. My son's done enough." Younkin thought about the yellow envelope tucked away in the desk and the one hundred twenty-five dollars it contained. Money Tom had loaned them to buy the mules. "I won't go to Tom again. We've already drained him."

Abe closed his eyes. His chest heaved and his head nodded in defeated acceptance.

Younkin's chin lowered to his chest. Tom had more saved in his bank account, but he could not go begging to his son once more. Tom had his own family to provide for. He did not need the burden of two old men who were incapable of making a go of it on their own anymore.

The room's heaviness inched closer with its weighted confinement. His body sagged beneath the unseen oppression. All men faced failures. Both Abe and he had ridden out their share. But this . . . there was something about this, a finality that offered no avenue of escape.

Younkin pushed from the tack box and crossed the room to the rolltop desk. He bent over, opened the lower drawer, and pulled out the bottle of bourbon hidden at the back. The cork came out of the bottle's mouth with a hollow, sucking sound.

Behind him, Abe cleared his throat. Younkin held his breath, waiting for a reprimand, but his friend said nothing.

Younkin studied the bottle and the amber liquor that gently rolled within. Nearly a month had passed since his last drink. It had not been easy, but there seemed to be a reason for leaving the bottle in the drawer. Now . . .

He lifted the bottle, placed its mouth to his lips, and swallowed. Sweet and burning, the bourbon cascaded down his throat to settle warmly in his stomach. He swallowed again, easier this time. The third came almost as an afterthought.

A knock rattled the tack room door on its hinges. "Jess? You in there, Jess?"

Younkin recorked the bottle and dropped it back into the drawer while Abe answered the door. Hank Wells poked his head inside. "There's a soldier fellow that wants to see you over at the office. Tom told me to come fetch you."

"Say what he wanted?" Younkin grabbed hat and coat from their wall pegs. Hank shook his head. With a shrug to Abe, Younkin followed Wells from the stable toward the sheriff's office.

"This lieutenant's got five other soldiers camped on the edge of town," the deputy said when they reached the office door. "He seems mighty anxious to meet you."

Without an answer, Younkin entered his son's office. The army officer sat with Frank Galvin and Tom around the stove. He stood when he saw Younkin. Despite a fine layer of dust on his blue coat and khaki breeches, he looked spit-and-polish Army.

"Mister Jess Younkin?" Younkin nodded and shook the soldier's hand when he pulled off a glove and extended it. "Lieutenant James Bishop, sir. My men and I have been sent from Fort Sill in reference to this."

Bishop dug into his coat and produced a yellow piece of paper that he handed to Younkin. Holding it at arm's length, Younkin scanned the message. It was the telegram he had sent to the fort last month.

"My superiors verified all you mentioned in the telegram. They reported you had an exemplary record as a scout during the Comanche campaign here in Texas." Bishop's manner was too formal for his years; twenty-four at the most, Younkin estimated. "I've come to enlist your aid in our endeavor."

"Tracking down Black Hand, huh?" Younkin chuckled. From the corner of an eye he caught the surprised expression on Wells's and Galvin's faces. Tom looked a bit shocked also.

"My assignment is to apprehend four Indians who escaped the Fort Sill reservation after killing two guards. I am to return them to the fort where they will stand trial for murder," Bishop explained. "I am to persuade you to ride with us as a scout and advisor, sir."

"Army ways must've changed a mite since I scouted for Mackenzie." Younkin grinned at the blond-haired officer while he tried to contain the trembling that quivered through him. "The Army used to offer a man more than words of persuasion for his services."

Perplexed, Bishop's jaw dropped an inch. "Sir, do I understand you expect monetary compensation for your services?"

"A fair day's wages for a fair day's work," Younkin answered without batting an eye. "Three hundred dollars in advance and expenses. For that, the Army'll get two men, myself and Abe Potter. Abe rode as a master sergeant with Mackenzie."

"Sir, surely you jest. I'm not discussing a business venture, but the apprehension of four murderers loose in this state. It's your civic duty—"

"Three hundred in advance and expenses." Younkin held the lean officer with his gaze.

"Sir, I—I don't believe . . ." Bishop fell silent as though unable to cope with the unexpected proposition. Finally, he sucked at his teeth and shrugged. "I haven't the authority to authorize such an expenditure. I'll have to telegraph Fort Sill."

"You do that, Lieutenant." Younkin suppressed the urge to grin when he turned to the door, feeling every eye in the room on him. The ploy had not worked yet, but if . . . He refused to consider that *if*. All he could do was wait and see. "When you get your answer, you can find me across the street at the stable."

Younkin eased back in his chair and studied the voucher Lieutenant Bishop handed him. It was not the same as gold or greenbacks, but it would suffice. He passed the slip of paper to Abe.

"Take it over to the bank, then make sure everyone gets their share." Younkin watched Abe inch his hat back and grin as he read the voucher.

"Think I'll do just that. If you gentlemen will excuse me, I have business to attend to." Abe pulled the limp-brimmed hat back atop his head and left the tack room.

Bishop watched the exit, then turned to Younkin. "Is that the Abe Potter who will assist us?"

"One and the same." Younkin nodded.

"A colored?" Bishop's tone contained undisguised contempt.

"A former buffalo soldier, Lieutenant. They were all black men." Younkin held back the irritation that sought to creep into his voice. "Whites like to forget we used the blacks to fight the Indian wars for us. Same as Texians forget Mexicans died fighting Santa Anna at the Alamo along with white men. Abe's not much of a business partner, worries like an old woman. But he's a good man. Forgot more about Comanches than most men ever knew."

Bishop stiffened and glanced away from the older man.

Younkin smiled, his reprimand striking the desired chords. "I believe we've business to get down to, Lieutenant."

The officer came to life. He eased a leather packet from his blue coat, opened it, and spread a map of Texas on the desk before Younkin. "Two days were lost waiting for that voucher to arrive. I hope you can provide a method to make up that lost time, Mister Younkin."

"We'll see what we can do." Younkin's attention turned to the detailed, three-color map.

"The best we can determine is the Indians crossed the Red River here in Wichita County." Bishop's finger touched the northern section of the map and slid southeast toward Dallas. "We lost their trail, then picked it up again near Bowie. They killed a steer for food about here."

Bishop's fingertip continued to move in a zigzag path into North Central Texas while he recounted other reports of slaughtered mules and steers. "It's believed they crossed the East Fork of the Trinity River here, near the small community of Crandall. A man was killed when some horses were stolen from his ranch, a Jack Garrison. Garrison's companion, who was rendered unconscious by a blow to the head, awoke to discover a sooty handprint on his forehead."

"Black Hand's work," Younkin confirmed.

"And grand stupidity. He marks his path like a man blazing a trail in the wilderness. Can't understand why this Toohmah would do anything so foolhardy." Bishop glanced at the older man.

"Black Hand isn't a white man. Taking coup is a matter of pride with him. He flaunts his ability in the face of the white man's authority," Younkin replied. "Don't underestimate him."

"It still appears to be grand stupidity to me." Bishop's expression was one Younkin had seen on a thousand white faces, that of the "natural" superiority of white over red.

"That might be, Lieutenant. But then, Black Hand is still running free, and no matter how he marks his trail the Army hasn't been able to track him down." An ironic smile twisted the corners of Younkin's lined mouth.

"A situation you and Abe Potter have been paid three hundred dollars to remedy, Mister Younkin." Bishop covered the barbs Younkin sank home with a mask of military efficiency. The officer returned to the map. "For a while, we were certain the four intended to ride south and cross the border into Mexico."

Bishop described the ransacking of a general store on the outskirts of Waco. Rifles, ammunition, food, and whiskey had been taken. "Two days later, a farmer and his hired hand were killed to the northwest, near Johnson Station. Since then, there have been no reports of the four."

"Black Hand won't be heading north or south. He's been leading the Army on a merry chase." Younkin's finger backtracked westward along the snaking line that represented the Brazos River. "I'd lay odds that he and his band are camped somewhere along the Brazos at this very moment. The Comanches used to make camps along its banks."

"Then we should ride eastward along the Brazos?" Bishop asked.

"We'll never chase Black Hand down. We've got to get ahead of him and let him come to us." Younkin leaned back in his chair. "Though you might alert all the local authorities along the river. By accident, they could stumble on the band."

Younkin pointed to the map. Starting high in the Texas Panhandle, he roughly traced the outline of the Texas Caprock. "From here west is the *Llano Estacado*, the Staked Plains. This was the home of the *Quahadi* band of the *Kwerharrehnuh* Comanches. Black Hand is *Quahadi*; he's coming home."

"Why? It doesn't make sense. In Mexico he would be free." Bishop's brow wrinkled in confusion.

"Black Hand's Comanche, and this was his people's land." *He's as old as I am. There's no place else for him to go,* Younkin wanted to add, but realized Bishop was too young to understand the stirrings that churned in the breasts of old men. "I suspect he'll follow the Brazos, then cut south before he reaches the caprock to confuse anyone on his trail. Then he'll head north again, backtracking before he rides up the caprock onto the High Plains."

"Where do you propose we 'get ahead of him'?" Bishop's gaze roved over the western sector of the map.

Younkin jabbed a finger below the dot that represented Lubbock, a town just below the Panhandle and near the southern edge of the caprock. "Here. It's rough country just off the caprock. Quanah Parker and his war bands used to camp among a series of gullies in this area when they returned from a raid to the south. Black Hand knows the terrain . . . as do I. He'll come there."

Younkin neglected to mention that when he last met Black Hand among those arroyos, the Comanche brave had left him staked naked atop an anthill in the summer sun. Abe and an Army patrol had found him, eyes clamped shut against the red ants. Swollen welts covered his body from the insects' fiery bites. He had lasted five hours in the unrelenting heat before the rescue.

The Tonkawa scout who had ridden with him was found a half-mile away. He, too, was staked to the ground naked. He had not been as lucky. A war lance had been driven through his chest, his dark mane peeled from his skull, and his genitals cut from his body and stuffed into his mouth.

"On my superiors' instructions, Mister Younkin, I am to follow your suggestions until they prove wrong." Bishop refolded the map and slid it back into its leather pouch. "It will take a day to gather the needed supplies, then we shall ride south and wait."

"We can leave in the morning." Younkin pushed from the desk and rose. "I had Jeb Barrett at the general store get supplies together the afternoon we first talked, Lieutenant. All your men have to do is pick them up."

Bishop stared at the older man in bewilderment for a moment, then nodded. "In the morning then, Mister Younkin."

After the officer left, Younkin took a yellow envelope containing a hundred twenty-five dollars from the desk and stuffed it in his coat pocket. He smiled at the thought of dropping it unopened on his son's desk. He savored the satisfaction that glowed warmly where only an icy desolation had dwelled for far too long.

Glancing around the tack room, he mentally made a list of all the things that needed to be done. He shook his head. There was two days' work that had to be completed in one afternoon to prepare for the morning. But before he started, there was the envelope to return.

He opened the tack room's door and stepped out into the West Texas winter. He whistled an off-tune version of "De Camp Town Races" while he crossed Main Street to the sheriff's office. The song flowed in part from sheer relief and in part from a newfound pride in himself.

CHAPTER 8

January 16, 1904

A deer, antlered head poised to sniff the scents carried in the air, stepped from behind a line of cedars. A soft whistling moved within the afternoon breeze, terminating in a solid thud.

Startled, the buck leaped. It hung in the air, delicate legs outstretched in a graceful arch. A shudder ran through its sleek brown body as the death that had pierced its heart an instant before now claimed its brain. The deer collapsed in midair and crumpled to the rocky ground. For a moment it twitched spasmodically, then lay still. Blood-tinted froth lathered its tapered mouth.

A self-satisfied smile uplifted Toohmah's leathery lips when he stepped from behind the live oak that had concealed him. The single arrow had flown true, striking below the left shoulder and driving straight to the heart quickly and cleanly. Tonight he would taste real meat, not the bland flesh of a white man's steer.

The old *Nermernuh* lifted the buck to his shoulders. Its lightness surprised him. His smile grew to a grin as he began the three-mile walk to the camp. It was not the deer's lack of weight, but his own increased strength that diminished the burden. For the first time since Quanah's surrender at Fort Sill, Toohmah felt alive, a whole man.

Even the past week of living on roots and nuts his companions and he managed to scrounge from the earth had not lessened the newly rediscovered strength. While Quinne, Chana, and Boisa Pah often complained of the hardships, he relished them. They were but reminders of harder times; times he had cursed in his youth, but pined for since the soldiers had penned him on the reservation like an animal. He was once again *Nermernuh*. His spirit walked the path that once all the People trod.

The soldiers still followed. Of that, he was certain. Boisa Pah had killed four Whites during their erratically twisting flight, and his own coup marks would assure the soldiers they remained on the right trail. Yet Toohmah held no fear. The great hunt only sharpened his senses, bringing a clarity that had not been in his mind in twenty-eight *taum*.

And he held true to his medicine vision. He had not killed or taken a scalp. He remained shielded from the double-edged knife that could sever his own life cord.

Exhilarated by the feel of the moment, he breathed deeply to taste the fragrance of the crisp winter air. He froze. The sharpness of burning cedar invaded his nostrils. For an instant, he thought his companions had disregarded his commands and lit a fire to warm themselves. But the camp, hidden along the serpentinely meandering banks of the Brazos, lay two miles away.

Voices came from his right. Toohmah's head jerked around. Ice flowed in his veins, while sweat prickled over his forehead. No more than twenty strides away, four white men sat crouched on their haunches about a small makeshift campfire. Their horses stood nearby, heads low to graze on a winter growth of needlegrass.

Toohmah sank to his knees behind the bushy cover of a cedar. His wandering thoughts and self-praise had almost led him right into their midst. Only an old fool could be so careless. Only his adherence to the *nenuhpee* warning had protected him. He stood downwind of the four so that not even the horses had detected his reckless approach.

"Off of it, boys. Time to get back to business." One of the men stood and threw the grounds from a coffeepot toward the cedar concealing Toohmah. The heavy aroma brought water to the warrior's mouth.

"Sheriff, I think those soldier boys with their telegram have lost their minds." Another man pushed up to kick sand over the low fire. "There ain't no Indians in these parts, or we'd have seen signs of them."

Soldiers? Telegram? Toohmah strained to hear the conversation.

"I've half a mind to agree with you, Hollis . . . if it weren't for the fact old man Lansdale caught sight of four riders in his north pasture night before last." The man placed the coffee pot in his saddlebags. "The Indians are killers. Wouldn't be right to have them riding through my county without taking them in."

"Rather we shot them, Sheriff," the one called Hollis said as the four mounted their horses. "Had to listen to my pa brag about fighting Comanche all my life. If we killed them four, maybe it would shut him up."

The four laughed and reined their horses westward. Toohmah released an overly held breath. Motionless, he waited until he no longer felt the vibration of the retreating hooves in the ground beneath him. Then he stood and hastened toward the east.

They cold-camped; the lack of fire seemed but a minor discomfort for Toohmah this night. The limestone cliff that rose from the Brazos' bank sheltered the site from the winter wind. Raw venison, still warm and bloody, bloated his belly. And he basked in the memory of the admiration that beamed on Quinne and Chana's faces while they gutted and skinned the buck. They had been hungry, and he had provided food. Their admiration was the honor garnered by the hunter.

"Old man, how did the soldiers know we are here?" Boisa Pah wiped the grease from his mouth with a shirt sleeve. "You told us our path would confuse them."

Toohmah's face remained expressionless. He could not display his own confusion to his companions. The soldier's telegraph message to the white sheriff warning him that the band rode through this country worried him. He could not fathom how the soldiers knew where they traveled. The path they journeyed had been wide and erratic. "It does not matter. Tomorrow we ride west along the river for five days. Then we ride south."

He attempted to quell his inner excitement. In ten days, they would camp at the foot of the great caprock. From there, they would move northward again for several days, following the caprock's base, before he once more walked the land of the *Quahadi*.

"We waste too much time," Boisa Pah replied. "The soldiers know we intend to ride west. Tomorrow, we should swing south to the Mexican border."

Closing his eyes, Toohmah gathered his strength. Each day Boisa Pah pushed harder for them to turn to the land of the *Mejanos*. Though the lanky brave had lost Chana's support, his demands grew more vocal. His arguments contained merit, perhaps even wisdom, Toohmah admitted to himself. However, the lands beyond the shallow Rio Grande meant nothing to the old brave.

"You, all of you, may ride south." Toohmah chewed a thin slice of venison. "I ride west with the sunrise."

"Toohmah has provided for us and led us wisely." Quinne wiped his hands on the thighs of his pants. "I will remain with my uncle."

"Dogs of the same spot run together." Boisa Pah grunted with disgust. He turned to Chana.

Nervously, the pig-faced youth glanced about him, his gaze eventually resting on his feet. Toohmah repressed the urge to sadly shake his head. The long, hard ride had only served to increase the indecision plaguing the young man's mind. Chana lacked the legs of a man and the strength to stand on them.

"I ride with Toohmah," Chana's answer came in a whisper.

"Old women waddling after an old man." Boisa Pah rose from where he squatted and walked away from his companions. Finding a bed of soft ground near an outcropping of limestone, he stretched out for the night.

"Ride south," Quinne called after the angular brave. "No one here will hinder you."

"Old women, bah!" Boisa Pah snorted, then rolled to his side, resting his head on an arm.

"He does not know the land or the ways of the hunter." Chana's head rose to Quinne and Toohmah. "He can not ride alone. He knows his ignorance would lead him into the Whites' hands."

Nor did the others have the knowledge needed for survival beyond the restrictions of the reservation, Toohmah realized. With time and experience, the three young men would learn to provide for themselves. He would show them the way. Until then, no matter how loud Boisa Pah's protests, he would remain leader of the small band. For despite their younger age, his mind and abilities gave him a strength they did not possess.

"You should rest, also. I will take the first watch," Toohmah said to the two at his side. "We ride hard tomorrow."

Without complaint, Quinne and Chana stood and selected ground for their beds. Toohmah sliced another strip of meat from the butchered deer at his feet. He placed the raw flesh in his mouth, not to quiet the rumblings of hunger but simply to savor the full flavor of its uncooked juices. In the morning, they would eat venison again. After that, days could pass before they tasted fresh meat. While he had hidden jerked beef, stolen from a rancher's smokehouse, in a saddlebag in the event the land failed to provide game, jerky could never fill a belly or bring the satisfaction of fresh-slain meat.

Toohmah's old eyes surveyed the land surrounding the camp. Silently, the Brazos flowed fifteen feet from where he sat on his heels. Across the river lay a wide clearing bordered by cedar and wind-gnarled red oaks that stood naked in the winter. The silvery moonlight cast a ghostly aura over the clearing, while their camp lay in the cliff's dark shadow.

The clearing held the aged warrior's attention as lodestone captures iron. While well hidden, ill fortune hovered over that small plot of land. How many *taum* had passed since he had last camped within its deceptive security? He could not remember the exact passing of the winters. An emptiness, the sense of something precious now lost, opened within his heart.

An ice floe raced up his spine; gooseflesh rippled on his arms. He cocked his head to one side. The voices of the dead seductively called to him, their coy promises whispers on the night wind. They summoned him, offering the eternal rest beyond life.

Toohmah shook himself, then listened again. There were no voices, only the rustle of wind among the dry grass. His eyes narrowed to slits and his brow furrowed. Had the whisperings been his imagination? Or had the voices merely ceased their urgings for the moment? What did a man know of the invisible powers that shared the world he walked?

On the surface, the clearing lay peaceful and inviting. Such were the illusions of appearance, which was the reason Toohmah had chosen to camp on the bank opposite the ill-fated clearing. It could not be trusted. The shades of those who died there dwelt in its rocks, trees, and grass, crouched and waiting to snare the soul of a man foolhardy enough to tread on the haunted ground.

Coyotes yapped in the distance, then broke into mournful wails that floated upward through the sky to the Moon Mother. Toohmah's inward wails echoed those of his wild brothers.

Thirty-three comings and goings of winter's ice, he remembered now, had passed, and still he found sorrow weeping within him. The clearing awoke long-buried memories, brought them to the surface of his thoughts and focused them with crystal clarity. Thirty-three years since he had last camped in the clearing. It seemed like the passing of a few short hours.

Why the Antelope Eaters had journeyed so far east that spring was forgotten now. It was of little importance. But everything else about that morning stood in his mind with the sharpness of a keenly honed knife edge.

He had awakened and tossed aside his buffalo robe to greet the brisk chill of morning. The space beside him was empty. He had smiled with pleasure. Such was the place of a woman, to rise before her husband.

Outside his tipi stood fifty tipis, smoke lazily rising from their tops. A few of the People moved through the camp, mostly women preparing the morning's meal for their men. Among them worked his wife. In the green grass at her feet played their two-year-old son.

After all the years, Toohmah repressed the names, never allowing them to intrude into his consciousness. To speak the names of the dead, to even remember them, was taboo to the *Nermernuh.* Yet, he recalled every other detail about the woman for whose hand he had paid thirty horses to her father.

He could feel the warmth of her flesh against his own as they lay together, see the joy in her smile, hear the sound of her voice, soft like a spring breeze weaving through buffalo grass. Long had he waited before taking a wife into his tipi, using instead his brothers' wives to quell the aching of his loins as was the custom of the People. Only this young woman, lithe and graceful as a doe, had captured his heart and spirit. Had her father asked, Toohmah would have given sixty ponies to win her as a bride.

She tossed back her waist-length, raven-black hair, braided with beads and bits of colored glass, and smiled widely when she saw him. She came to him and hugged him tightly in an open display of love and affection common among the *Nermernuh.*

"A new seed was planted within me last night," she whispered into his ear. "My husband is a mighty warrior and a mightier lover. Soon I shall bear him another son."

Toohmah crushed her to him. His pleased laughter echoed up and down the banks of the Brazos. He did not doubt her pronouncement. The ways of women were mysterious, perhaps even more powerful than the magic medicine men garnered about them. Had she not told him when they conceived their first son?

Kissing his cheek, she extracted herself from his arms. "Now I must prepare my husband a hearty meal. He will need to gather his strength today. Tonight our bodies will revel in one another for long hours to celebrate the life we have created."

She tauntingly turned from him and walked back to their son and her work. Filled with the joy of new life, Toohmah sang as he strutted proudly through the camp. The eyes of the older women lifted from their morning tasks when he passed. They shook their heads at his foolishness and laughed softly among themselves. He paid them no heed. In nine months, a new son would announce his presence to the band with his wailing cries.

Lost in the pleasure of the new morning, he left the clearing and strolled through the forest of cedar and budding red oaks. Today, he would hunt. Rabbit, deer, antelope, none would escape his arrows. His chest swelled at the thought of his wife's pride when he reconfirmed that he was a good provider for their family, that no other brave among the *Quahadi* could offer her more. There would be a celebration, and they would feed those in the band who had no meat to fill their pots.

A mile from the camp, he stopped and squatted by the river. He cupped his palms into the cold water and raised his hands to his lips.

The bugle of the buffalo soldiers tore through the morning's stillness. Then the thundering crack of rifles.

He ran. Like the bounding namesake of the band, he raced along the river bank. When he arrived at the clearing, the fight was over. It had lasted no more than minutes. Two bluecoats lay dead and ten of the Comanche band. Among those claimed by the soldiers' bullets were his wife and son; their scalps had been cut from their heads.

Toohmah sucked in a deep breath, attempting to alleviate the old pains that had awakened. They would not leave, nor would the image of the grinning white scout who flaunted the hair of his wife and child from across the river. He had sought the name of the man at every meeting of the Comanche bands until he had learned it—Jess Younkin.

That day in the clearing was but their first meeting. Once Toohmah thought he had killed the scout, leaving him staked atop a mound of red ants, his naked body smeared with honey. Yet Younkin had survived and lived to witness Quanah's surrender at Fort Sill.

The day Toohmah had taken coup on the scout. Amid the defeat of his people, his chest had swelled with pride in that last victory. Now, it seemed as empty and hollow as the curse he had spit in Younkin's face. In all the years that separated him from that moment, he had prayed that the white scout had found a death that robbed his soul of eternal happiness.

The crunch of gravel beneath foot came from behind the aged brave. Toohmah cast a glance over a shoulder. Quinne approached and squatted beside him.

"I thought that I had caught you napping, Uncle." Quinne smiled with affection.

"I have never slept on watch." Toohmah's words were terse and contained an edge he had not meant for the son of his sister's daughter.

For long moments, they sat silently. Toohmah felt pride for the young man. In Quinne, he found a son to replace the one stolen from him in the clearing thirty-three *taum* ago. Even as a child, Quinne had listened, hungry to learn the ways of the *Nermernuh*. Had Toohmah's son lived to manhood, the old brave thought, he would have been as strong and wise as Quinne. No man could wish for more.

"Is Boisa Pah right?" Quinne swallowed as though the question came hard. "Should we ride to Mexico?"

Toohmah nodded. "It would be safer and easier."

Again, Quinne sat in silence for heavy minutes. "Then why do we journey to the west?"

The frosty moonlight played over the youthful features of Quinne's face. Toohmah studied them, trying to delve beneath the surface. Would he understand? Could the things that moved within the old touch youth? Quinne had proven himself a man during their flight; he had become a brave. He deserved an answer that hid nothing.

"I grow old. Little time is left to me." Toohmah hesitated, pondering the correct words. "Before that time is gone, I must feel the soil of the High Plains beneath my feet once more. It will make the leaving of this earth easier."

Whether he understood or not, Quinne answered, "Then I will walk the plains beside you, Uncle."

Toohmah touched the young man's shoulder and smiled. He then rose and walked back among the shadows, lying down where Quinne had slept but moments ago. The watch left to the son of his sister's daughter, he closed his eyes and escaped the ghosts of the past that surrounded him.

CHAPTER 9

January 26, 1904

Younkin let the buckskin come to a halt on its own atop a low-running hogback ridge. The gelding's head dropped to a dry clump of feather grass that pushed from the rocky soil. While his mount grazed, Younkin's fingers caressed the scarred briar pipe nestled in his coat pocket. He decided against the long-burning bowl and pulled a sack of tobacco from his shirt to roll a cigarette.

"Texas weather! Makes a man think the Lord lost his mind when he created this country." Abe, astride a roan filly, shed his coat and draped it across the saddle horn. "Must be close to seventy today. Hell, there was ice in my canteen this morning. If a man isn't scorched to death during the day, he'll freeze at night."

"Texas weather," Younkin repeated with a chuckle. He remembered his parents telling him about a sign that earlier settlers had placed at a ford across the Red River. Bearing an arrow that pointed to Texas, the sign read, THIS WAY TO HELL.

A southwest wind blew into Younkin's face. He felt the hint of moisture it carried up across Baja and Mexico from the Pacific Ocean. "If this keeps up, we could get some rain. Rain or not, reckon we're in for a warm spell for a few days."

"Or a month. Or it will drop below freezing in the next ten minutes. Only a madman would try to outguess the weather in this country . . . only a madman." Abe cocked an eyebrow high as he looked at his friend. "What're you grinning at? You look like a cowhand who just paid his first visit to a Juárez cathouse."

"Feel good." Younkin stuck the twisted end of the cigarette between his lips. While he dug a match from a pocket, he passed the tobacco to Abe. "It's the warmth. Feels like spring's come early."

The white-haired black skeptically eyed Younkin while he stripped off his own coat. "Ain't no warmth making you grin like a jackass. It's being here, acting like the past twenty years never happened."

Younkin took a long draw from the cigarette without answering. Abe's observation contained more truth than he had admitted to himself. It was good to be here.

"If it weren't for that three hundred dollars, you wouldn't find me here. My ass is too old and bony to sit atop a horse all day. And my back isn't cut out for sleeping on hard ground." Abe grunted while he lit his cigarette. "But you'd be here no matter what. If the Army hadn't shelled out the three hundred, you'd have volunteered. Just itching to try your hand at an old Indian who should've died and blown away years ago."

"Abe, you talk too much to ever make a good scout." His friend was wrong. Clara and their life together had taken the old hate and bitterness out of him. Black Hand was no more than a vague nightmare that belonged to a young man he barely remembered. But being here . . .

"You still ain't got nothing to be grinning about," Abe continued, ignoring Younkin. "You might have convinced a wet-behind-the-ears lieutenant you know what you're doing, but I'm not so sure. We've been here five days, and there's still no sign of Black Hand."

"He'll be here." Younkin clucked the buckskin into a leisurely walk. Below the ridge, the reds and browns of the eroded terrain rolled like lazy water for as far as the eye could see, the monotony occasionally broken by sparse green patches of winter needlegrass. There was no trace of Black Hand and the three young braves who rode with him. Doubt niggled at the back of Younkin's mind. "He'll be here. All we have to do is wait him out."

"A couple more days and you'll have a hard time convincing Bishop of that fact." Abe nudged the roan after his friend. "He's getting restless."

"Black Hand will be here," Younkin repeated as much for himself as for Abe.

He could feel it. Black Hand *would* be here. The Comanches were ruled by habit, an arrogant people often trapped by their own wiles. During his time as a scout, they had forever underestimated the whites and their ability to strike deep into the heart of the High Plains. If the Comanche had not, Mackenzie never would have caught them in Palo Duro Canyon.

Younkin doubted that time had changed Black Hand, or his contempt for whites. That and the fact that he would get reckless the closer he came to the caprock was what the scout gambled on. There was nothing like the feeling that a man was safe at home to make him relax and start making mistakes. Younkin's job was to be there when the old brave made those mistakes.

"Ain't going to say anything else, are you?" Abe edged his mount beside his friend.

"Nope." Younkin leaned down to stub out the cigarette butt on a boot sole and flicked it away.

Again he surveyed the rugged terrain below their position. The gullies formed a maze that fanned out for miles. A lone man who kept low could hide for weeks among the winding wounds in the earth. But Black Hand was not alone. He rode with three young bucks who would be as impatient as Bishop and his troopers back at camp. And impatient men tend to be accident-prone.

"You smell something?" Abe interrupted Younkin's train of thought. Younkin took a deep breath and shook his head. Abe slowly sucked in the wind through his nose once again. "Must be my imagination. Thought I got a whiff of something burning . . . grass maybe. Don't smell it now."

"Probably the cigarette. It's not like good pipe tobac . . ." Younkin's words trailed into silence. He caught a whiff of something. His nostrils flared while he drew in a long breath.

It was there, a coy trace of smoke like a small fire that burned miles away.

Unlooping a pair of binoculars from his saddle horn, Younkin meticulously searched the land. He completed one circle and began the circuit again.

"Anything?" Abe asked.

"No . . ." Younkin blinked, uncertain whether he had seen it. He moved the binoculars back. There! No more than a waver in the air. "Yes . . . by God . . . yes."

"What?"

Like the quavering waves of radiating heat from sun-baked sand that produced watery mirages, it rose in a thin column no more than a mile away. "It's a small fire. The air's shimmying just above the ground."

Abe took the offered binoculars and peered in the direction of Younkin's pointing finger. "Got it, but I don't see a fire. Should be able to make it out from here. The ground looks flat."

Younkin smiled as he took the binoculars back. He glanced around. A quarter of a mile ahead, the ridge abruptly jutted upward in a steep rise. "Let's take a look from up there."

Aware that other eyes might be watching their movements from below, Younkin reined the buckskin behind the ridge to conceal their movement. Halfway down the gentle slope, he halted. Dismounting, he tied the horse to a mesquite sapling. Younkin turned to the steep rise.

Abe swung down from the filly, his gaze following Younkin's. "This ain't a job for two old men."

Younkin grinned at his friend's complaints and began the climb. Ten minutes later, the two lay on their bellies atop the crest. Younkin peered through the binoculars, then passed them to Abe. "Take a look."

"I'll be damned." A soft whistle escaped Abe's puckered lips when he lowered the binoculars and handed them back to Younkin.

Pleased, the aged scout took one more look below. The change in position had provided the vantage point he had hoped for. The ground was not as flat as it first appeared. It opened in a deep arroyo. Within the wind- and water-cut scar, four men huddled about a small campfire over which roasted two rabbits. While they were dressed in white men's clothing, the long gray hair that trailed down one of the men's back was inescapable. It was Black Hand.

"You haven't changed, you old bastard." Younkin spoke in a whisper to the brave below. The fire was the mistake he had been praying for. "I knew you'd come. I knew it."

Lieutenant Bishop slowly lowered his binoculars. The cynical expression he had worn a moment before vanished from his youthful face. He smiled at Younkin. "I must apologize for the doubts I've harbored, Mister Younkin. It appears my superiors were correct in their estimation of your abilities."

Younkin offered no reply but inwardly basked in the unexpected compliment. Bishop glanced overhead and sucked at his teeth. Only the red afterglow of sunset remained in the sky.

"Gentlemen, I feel it is too late to take action this evening. We'll ride in and take them at daybreak," Bishop pronounced with authority.

Behind the young officer, Younkin saw Abe pucker his lips and roll his eyes as though to say, "What did you expect?" Younkin tilted his head toward the arroyo. "Lieutenant, I don't think riding down on those four is too wise."

Bishop arched an eyebrow. "Mister Younkin?"

"Black Hand will spot us before we reach the foot of this hill," Younkin explained. "They'd be long gone before we arrived at their camp. I, for one, don't relish having to chase them down—that is, *if* we could."

"Have you a better suggestion?" Bishop's tone was skeptical.

Younkin squinted against the dusk. "The walls of the arroyo are steep. No horse can climb them. Black Hand's got careless; he's boxed himself in. Close the mouth of the gully, and they're trapped inside."

Bishop edged back the brim of his hat. "We move in during

the night, close off the arroyo, and capture them in the morning?"

"It would be better if we could manage it all at night, but that would be pressing our luck," Abe answered. "Doubt if we could get that close without waking them. And if it comes down to a fight, like as not we'd end up shooting one another in the dark."

"Are you implying my men can't tell those Indians from—" Bishop frowned with indignation.

"Abe's not implying anything, Lieutenant. He's trying to avoid accidents." Younkin tried to soothe ruffled feathers.

Bishop made no reply but sat silently. Abe rolled his eyes and shook his head.

"Lieutenant, I have one more suggestion." Younkin took a deep breath and hoped for the best. "There's a ranch fifteen miles north of here owned by a man named Norwood. He usually keeps about ten hands on payroll to help run his stock. If Abe or I were to ride out now, we could have those men back here before you moved on Black Hand."

Disbelief clouded Bishop's face. "Sir, first Potter implies my men are incapable of telling themselves from four heathens, and now you suggest they aren't capable of capturing these Indians without civilian aid."

"Maybe they are, and maybe they aren't. But I'd rather weight the odds in our favor." Younkin maintained his composure, despite his growing irritation. Though twenty-eight years had passed since he had last served as a scout, the military mentality had not changed. "With another ten men, we could surround—"

"Forget it, Mr. Younkin. I refuse to be responsible for the welfare of civilians. I don't want a military operation transformed into a turkey shoot," Bishop replied. "As Potter said, we will be pressing our luck by taking our positions during the night as it is."

"We'll be pressing it a mite more if we don't get Norwood and his hands." Younkin sensed Bishop's military stubbornness stiffen his backbone to an unyielding rail of steel. "Black Hand's a tricky bastard. Leave him an opening, no matter how small, and he's liable to wiggle through it. With extra men, we'd make sure there aren't any openings."

"Mister Younkin," Bishop glared at him, "my superiors assigned me a detail of five men with which to apprehend those four Indians. With you two and me, that is a total of eight men, a number that should be more than sufficient to deal with the situation."

"What should be isn't always the way of things, Lieutenant." Younkin found it increasingly more difficult to contain his anger. "I've dealt with Black Hand before. I've seen him and ten braves outwit Mackenzie and a whole troop of buffalo soldiers. You're not dealing with whites. Those four are Comanches."

"We're dealing with escaped murderers, nothing more, nothing less. If I were to accept your proposal to solicit civilian aid, and if word of it ever found its way back to Fort Sill, I'd never be able to live—" Bishop caught himself. He looked away from Younkin. "I'll not send for a band of untrained cowboys."

The truth had finally surfaced. Younkin no longer held back his anger. His voice deepened, grating harshly. "Damn it, Lieutenant! You're not thinking. You're sitting here worrying about what it would look like on your record if you asked for outside help. Meanwhile, you're leaving yourself open. What's it going to look like if you let those four get away?"

"I've made my decision, Mister Younkin." Bishop rose and started down the hill. "I'll hear no more on the subject. No more."

"Damn!" Younkin kicked a rock at his feet to vent his frustration. "The stubborn bastard. He doesn't understand that's Black Hand out there, not some decrepit, drunken Indian."

"All officers are stubborn bastards." Abe pushed to his feet. "It's going to be a long night."

CHAPTER 10

January 27, 1904

Crouched low in the early-morning darkness, Younkin edged along the western lip of the arroyo. His breath came low and steady, yet it resounded like a roaring bellows in his head. Each step was slow and deliberate, the soles of his round-toed boots placed flat on sand or grass to avoid the crunch of rocks that lay washed bone-white in the moonlight. The uncontrollable pounding of a hammer on an anvil reverberated in his chest and raced upward to fill his temples. His palms, slick with sweat when he started, were unnaturally dry. A persistent itching nagged at the heels of both hands.

Fear; he faced the doubt that writhed within him. Sixty years had not eliminated the fear. The exhilaration of the chase, the hunt, always ended in the fear, the realization that life could end in the next moment, the result of some overlooked detail, a foolish mistake. The fear could be contained, but never conquered.

A quarter of a mile from where he had left Lieutenant Bishop and the troopers at the mouth of the wash, Younkin sank closer to the ground. He swung the muzzle of the Winchester he clutched in both hands to cover the eroded gash that opened in the earth to his left. Fifteen feet below, four men slept, nestled close together to share their body warmth in the cold night.

Younkin inched closer, rifle ready should any of the four awake to discover the intruder who stalked above them. He required no more than a single glance to confirm their identities, yet he sat back on his heels and peered down. His attention focused on the old man, who lay on his back. Time had done much to alter that face bathed in the moon's silver light. But there was no mistaking it. The sagging mouth, the heavy, weathered lines of age, could not disguise the countenance of a younger brave who had left him for dead staked atop an anthill.

Younkin lifted the Winchester to his shoulder. He sighted dead center of the sleeping Comanche's forehead. His finger tightened around the trigger.

So easy, he realized, to simply squeeze gently. One shot would end a chase that had begun more than half a lifetime ago. One bullet would close the door on a portion of his life that had remained open and unsettled for forty years.

Younkin's body went slack. Cold sweat prickled over him.

The rifle lowered, muzzle ever ready if needed. Younkin closed his eyes and softly drew in a steadying breath and released it. Confusion clouded his mind. Something within him, something that evaded rational thought and definition, prevented him from pulling the trigger. His finger refused to curl that last fraction of an inch, to close the open door of his past.

Once there would have been no hesitation. He would have taken all four while they slept, grateful for catching a band of Comanches unawares.

Now? He did not know. He had no doubt he could kill the braves before they reacted to his first shot. It would be cleaner and quicker than waiting for sunrise and attempting to capture them. But something was wrong with ending all those years with four quick shots. That something eluded the aged scout while eating away at him at the same time.

Mentally cursing his reluctance, Younkin backed away from the arroyo for a hundred paces. He paused an instant, unable to pull his gaze from the gully. Then he pivoted and in a crouched run returned to the entrance to the arroyo and the soldiers positioned across its mouth.

Abe and Bishop moved to his side as he sank to the soft sand and tried to regain his breath. "It's them."

"Are you positive?" Bishop questioned. Younkin felt the officer tense.

"No doubt. It's Black Hand and the young bucks," Younkin assured him. "They're asleep a quarter-mile up the wash. Didn't even have a man keeping watch. I moved in close enough to see Black Hand's face."

Bishop turned to face the arroyo's mouth. "Then all we have to do is wait for the sun."

Abe leaned close to his friend, his voice barely audible. "You had me worried, Jess. I thought you would kill them on your own."

"So did I," Younkin said. "So did I."

"Aayy aayy ayyy ayy aayy," the cry tore from Toohmah's chest and throat in a high-pitched yap. He grinned widely with relish. "Aayy ayy aayy ayy aayy."

The pressure of his bare thighs and heels squeezed the pinto's sides. The pony lunged inward toward the thundering brown mass of the buffalo herd. Above the deep drumming of cloven hooves, Toohmah heard the other braves of the *Quahadi* band shout at the beasts, driving them in a wild stampede across the open prairie.

Ahead of him, barely discernible through the clouds of throat-choking dust, the hind legs of a bay stallion flailed the empty air. A second later, the fallen horse and its rider were drowned in a sea of buffalo as the herd closed over them.

Toohmah tried to recall the bay and its rider. He could not, his mind was empty. The heat of the hunt raced through his veins and brain like a wind-whipped prairie fire. There was no moment to life beyond this. The herd was the first of the season. Later the band would count its losses. Now, only the kill mattered.

A great, hump-shouldered bull, froth spuming from its bellowing mouth, separated from the herd. It charged the pinto. Its shaggy head savaged at the horse and rider, curved horns intent on ripping the pony's belly wide.

Without breaking stride, the pinto shied to the side. The

bull's horns swept harmlessly through empty air, the pony remaining inches beyond range of the pointed death.

"Aayy aayy aayy ayyy," Toohmah screamed. He stretched the notched arrow back in his bow, gut string taut and strained. His fingers opened, releasing.

The arrow shot forward, covering the two feet that separated rider from bull faster than the eye could perceive. The razor-honed head, then the shaft, buried itself below the buffalo's right shoulder to burrow between ribs straight to the creature's heart.

The bull's head wrenched upward, horns once more seeking the pony. Again the savage attack missed its sweat-lathered target. The bull stumbled. Then it was over. The buffalo's forelegs buckled beneath him. Down, his great weight crumpled to the earth, his neck twisting at an unnatural angle as his body flew over his head.

"Aaayyy aayy aayyy." Toohmah yanked a second arrow from his quiver, ready for another kill. The bull would be found by the women and children who followed the braves on foot. Skinning and dressing the carcasses were their tasks. His prize would come that night when he gorged his belly on the hot, grease-dripping meat.

"Aayy ayy ayy . . ."

His hunting cry faded. Two stones clacked together somewhere in the night.

The old brave's eyes opened to thin slits. The youthful dream vanished down the corridor of memories. His hand tightened on the rifle at his side. *Chana?*

Toohmah glanced to his feet. The pig-faced young man lay asleep on the ground instead of standing guard, as had been his task. Toohmah cursed to himself. Such carelessness could cost them their lives were . . .

A shadow moved at the corner of an eye. He drew in a long, steady breath and exhaled likewise, imitating the rhythm of sleep.

The shadow edged to the lip of the arroyo. A man! Moonlight glinted along the barrel of a rifle as the lone figure stared into the eroded wash.

Toohmah's heart raced, pounding wildly as though trying to escape his chest. He fought the urge to cry out in warning to his companions. Instead he maintained his charade of sleep, his eyes slightly slit, breath deep and constant.

The rifle rose to the man's shoulder. Toohmah's brain screamed for him to lift his own rifle, swing its muzzle upward, and fire before the silent intruder could pull the trigger of his weapon. The old brave remained motionless. The *nenuhpee* warning held him. If he did not kill, his way would be free of danger.

Above, the rifle trembled; its barrel drooped. Before the tension eased from Toohmah's taut muscles, moonlight washed beneath the brim of the hat the shadow wore.

Younkin!

It could not be, yet it was. His most hated enemy, a man who should be dead, hovered above him like a buzzard in search of carrion. The face was lined and creased as the land surrounding them, but there was no doubt it belonged to the man who once scouted for the buffalo soldiers. The same man who had slaughtered Toohmah's wife and infant son.

The *nenuhpee* tested him beyond the strength of a mere man. Why the white man did not fire was incomprehensible to the Comanche. Were their places reversed, Toohmah would not have hesitated. He would have fired, screaming his curses into Younkin's face, laughing while the man died.

Toohmah's grip tightened around his rifle. To avenge the ghosts of his wife and son, to kill the army scout, only that would be worth forsaking the chance of walking the High Plains once more before death claimed his life.

Younkin backed away from the arroyo's edge. His footsteps were less than whispers as the night swallowed him. Toohmah lay on his back in the moonlight, listening until even imagined sounds faded from his ears. Then he rolled to Quinne. He placed a hand over the youth's mouth to stifle any noise, and nudged him. Quinne's eyes flew wide.

"Shhhh," Toohmah whispered. The eyes of the son of his sister's daughter rolled to him. "We have been found. Make no sound. I will wake the others."

Quinne nodded. Toohmah crawled from the youth's side and awoke the others. When the three younger men gathered before him, the old *Nermernuh* whispered, "There was a man above us. I fear he may be with others. Ready the horses quietly and wait here until I return."

Before they could question his intentions, the old brave rose and disappeared into the shadows that clung to the western side of the arroyo. The night hung still about the brave as he hugged the rock and dirt of the gully's wall and worked toward its mouth. Neither night birds nor coyotes offered their cries to the moon.

He stood less than a hundred strides from their position when he first saw them. Six men in soldiers' uniforms squatted in the sand across the arroyo's entrance.

Soldiers? The worst of Toohmah's fears were realized. He had no doubt that Younkin was responsible for leading them here, but how had the white scout brought them to this spot? Since leaving the banks of the Brazos, Toohmah had carefully concealed their trail. What had drawn Younkin to this place so far from the river?

The scout and another man stepped from the shadows and squatted among the soldiers. Was the other man a rancher who had sighted them and summoned the soldiers? What careless mistake had given away their camp?

The Comanche tried to clear his mind, to force the panicked bewilderment from his head. Nothing could be gained by pondering the unknown. The hows and whys did not matter. The soldiers were here—and they blocked the only avenue of escape from the arroyo.

Toohmah sank back toward his companions. He searched the wash's walls in desperation. Only near the mouth did their height drop enough for the horses to scale. He had been a fool. He had led the others into the inescapable confines of the arroyo. His brain reeled beneath the weight of his own stupidity. This land which once had been the domain of the People was now held by others. The secrets the land had only shared with the *Nermernuh* now belonged to the Whites.

Toohmah felt as naked and vulnerable as a newborn child.

The land had always sheltered the Comanche. The *Nermer-nuh* had defeated the invaders who sought to conquer this country. The Spanish, the Mexicans, the French, the English, the Texians, were held back for generations because the land had not revealed its secrets to them. The scarce water holes, the concealing imperfection of the terrain that could hide a brave or a band amid the open flatness of the prairie, all had belonged to the Comanches. Now the Whites shared those secrets. The land had abandoned the People. It had betrayed the old brave, cast him out, stripped away its powerful medicine.

Fear quaked through the aged warrior, a fear that did not stem from facing death, but a fear that came from the realization that he stood alone, severed from the life and traditions that guided his feet. He had not killed. He had remained faithful to the *nenuhpee* vision. How could this happen, to be trapped and killed like a frightened animal?

He *had not killed.* Truth rang at the heart of his panicked realization. The Little Folk had given him a path to follow, one he had never strayed from. Though the land betrayed him, he retained the promise of the vision. Had not Younkin lowered his rifle when he stood on the edge of the wash? Had not his faith in the vision brought them this far without serious injury? Even Chana's broken arm had not slowed their progress.

Confidence swelled to replace fear as Toohmah rejoined his three companions. The *nenuhpee* promise of safety still shielded him. A man needed no more.

"Well, old man?" Boisa Pah spoke.

"Soldiers wait at the mouth of the arroyo." Toohmah noticed Chana's eyes widen, but the pig-faced one did not squeal with fright. For that, the old brave gave silent thanks.

"And you led us into this trap!" Boisa Pah spat at Toohmah's feet.

Before the old brave could react, Quinne interceded. "What must we do now, Uncle?"

"The soldiers wait for sunrise to attack, or else we would

wear their chains at this moment," Toohmah answered. "While it is dark, we must ride through them."

"We could climb the walls," Boisa Pah said.

"How far could we make it on foot?" Toohmah felt the fear the three shared. "I did not see the soldiers' horses, but they cannot be far away. We would cover no more than a mile before they would run us down."

"We'll circle them on foot and kill them." Boisa Pah refused to concede to the older man.

"The sun will rise before we could circle them." Toohmah glanced at the moon hanging low on the western horizon. "Our horses and the darkness are our allies. We must use them."

The old warrior took his mount's reins from Quinne, tossed them around the horse's neck, and swung into the saddle. "Hug close to the west wall. Its shadow will cloak you. If fortune is with us, we can ride over the soldiers before they notice our presence. When I charge, lie low on your pony's neck. Use your horse as a shield."

He nudged his mount into the shadows.

Only Abe's soft breathing and an occasional cough muffled against an arm met Younkin's ears. Beyond a few feet, the sounds were indiscernible. Nothing stirred within the arroyo, not that he expected it to. The soldiers had taken position quietly and had remained that way. Overhead the night's darkness still dominated the sky. The eastern horizon was as black as the western heaven. The sun lay at least two hours away.

"I could use a smoke," Abe whispered at Younkin's side.

"Tried sucking on my empty pipe. It didn't help." Younkin's gaze remained fixed on the wash. "It's just the waiting."

They had taken position at the arroyo too early, he decided, then edged the thought away. Bishop had been right. Better to wait out the sunrise here than to attempt to sneak up as dawn approached. Still, he would feel more comfortable with the extra guns from Norwood's ranch.

Younkin studied the men fanned across the entrance to the

ravine. They stirred restlessly. He looked back to the arroyo, not wanting to read his own nervousness into their cramped muscles.

"You hear something?" Abe nudged his side.

Nothing moved down the moonlit center of the arroyo. Younkin shook his head. Even the coyotes were silent.

"I don't like it, Jess," Abe continued. "I've got a crawly feeling on the back of my neck I can't shake."

Did that shadow within a shadow on the west wall move? Younkin blinked and stared. He could not be certain. His eyes were tired. *Damn!* It did move. Something was there.

"Lieutenant . . ." The warning was never completed. Empty one moment, the arroyo contained four horses and riders in the next instant.

War cries rent the night's silence. The blue-and-yellow blazes of firing rifles tore holes in the darkness. Someone shouted a command to open fire. Immediately, the soldiers returned the attack. Younkin heard the high-pitched whines as the hasty volley ricocheted off the arroyo's walls in erratic flight. Undeterred, the four riders and their barking rifles still came.

Younkin hefted his rifle to his shoulder, taking careful aim on the nearest rider. To his right, a man screamed and jerked to his feet. From the corner of an eye, Younkin saw the man's violent twisting, the blur of his body as he fell. There was no time to dodge. The soldier collapsed into the scout, throwing Younkin's rifle muzzle into the sand. The Winchester went off, bullet harmlessly spent in the ground. Other cries rose over the ceaseless report of the riders' guns.

Younkin's head snapped up. He acted rather than thought. Arms wide, he leaped to the left, carrying Abe and himself out of the path of an oncoming horse.

The old scout rolled to his feet and groped for the rifle he had lost in the chaos. The effort was wasted. With a curse, he jerked a Colt .45 from the holster strapped to his leg. Too late: the four were already beyond pistol range. Two rifles cracked at his right, but the Comanches rode on.

"Sons of bitches." Abe pushed from the ground to stare after the escaping riders. "They knew we were here."

Younkin contained his own frustration, turning instead to the wounded trooper groaning at his feet.

CHAPTER 11

The sun rode above the horizon when Younkin and Abe reached the rise that overlooked the arroyo. The morning's warmth penetrated the scout's fleece-lined coat, edging away the last vestiges of the night's chill from his body. By noon, he would have no use for the coat. The day was going to be another unseasonably warm one.

As they walked around the base of the hill, neither man broke the silence they had carried with them since leaving Lieutenant Bishop at the wash. Occasionally, Younkin caught Abe's head turning to the east. He followed his friend's gaze over the barren terrain of muted reds and browns. The gesture was wasted; there was nothing to see. Black Hand and the three young braves had had ample time to flee beyond the range of the naked eye.

It would be easy to find their tracks, Younkin realized. He might be able to trail them for ten miles before the tracks abruptly vanished, leaving no trace of horses or riders. Tumbleweeds dragged behind horses could obliterate hoofprints from the dry, sandy soil. If a wind came up, Black Hand would not have to be bothered with such a simple precaution. Nature would cover his trail.

A curse rose from within Younkin's chest to lodge in his throat unuttered. Profanity, no matter how vehement, would not erase the attack. Had Bishop taken his advice and gotten the extra men from the Norwood ranch, Black Hand would be the Army's prisoner now, or dead. As with his own son, too many years separated Younkin from the young officer. Bishop refused to fully trust himself to an old man whose time was past. The scout's gaze lowered to the ground; he continued the long walk.

They found the horses, tied to a twisted mesquite, undisturbed behind the rise where they had been left earlier. Mounting his buckskin, Younkin gathered the reins of three of the other horses and waited while Abe climbed atop his roan and took the remaining mounts.

Younkin spurred his gelding up the hogback and halted on its crest. He noticed Abe give him a sidelong glance when he unstrung the binoculars from the saddle horn. His friend did not stop, but reined his filly down the gentle slope as though he realized Younkin's action was useless.

It was. The binoculars' increased visual range provided no trace of the Comanches. Not so much as a wisp of dust stirred the air. Securing the binoculars about the saddle horn, Younkin touched the buckskin's flanks with his spurs and moved after Abe.

"Damn it, Jess"—Abe's voice finally broke the self-imposed silence—"I'm too old for this sort of thing."

Younkin reined beside his friend. "We're both a bit rusty. Eight years can take the edge off a man."

"Eight years? Jess, I'm talking about sixty-two years. My edge hasn't been keen for a long time. Now there's no edge at all." Weariness seemed to weigh down Abe's words. "Men our age are supposed to sit around with grandchildren on their knees."

Younkin shook his head. "I'll admit we could have handled ourselves better this morning, but—"

"There ain't no buts about it. I handled myself like an old man. I'd've been run down if you hadn't shoved me out of the way." Abe paused. His body sagged. "Worse, I was scared. It's been eight years since I felt that. I didn't like feeling it again. Old age is a time when a man's supposed to be safe and secure, not staring at some loco brave set on trampling him beneath a horse."

"Is it any different from the way we've been living?" Younkin sighted the arroyo's mouth in the distance. "A crazy Comanche buck or a banker who'd take your life away if you're late on a debt . . . Appears to me they're one and the same. Give either the chance, and they'll kill you."

Abe's head twisted to his friend. An expression of puzzlement moved over the ebony lines of his face. "You weren't scared this morning, were you?"

"Happened too fast to be scared." Younkin realized for the first time that he had not felt fear during the attack. The aftermath of the skirmish had worked its way into his gut and knotted it. But the actual attack . . . He was unsure what he felt, if anything.

"Damn!" Abe glanced ahead, then looked back to the aged scout. "I guess I've been wanting that livery stable so bad that I've been blind to you. You've been running scared for eight years. The bank, the loan, the bills, they frighten you more than looking down the wrong end of a rifle barrel."

Younkin refused to consider the implications contained in Abe's accusation. Abe was a good friend, but he worried like an old spinster. He read too much into things.

"The whiskey, spinning all those tales for Jimmy, I just thought you were getting a bit senile." Abe chuckled. His expression contained no mirth. "It wasn't that at all. You were scared. It was easier to hide in a bottle and all the memories than try and make a go of the stable."

"The stable's still going." His friend's persistence irritated Younkin. "We're earning the money that's keeping it alive right now."

"The army money was dumb luck, and you know it." Abe's head moved sadly from side to side. "Dumb luck that kept us from losing the stable."

"Dumb luck? What about the telegram I sent to Fort Sill?"

"The three hundred didn't mean to you what it meant to me." Abe disregarded Younkin's protest. "The stable's my life, Jess. For eight years, I've sweated blood to make it work, to show the town an old nigger can make it in a white world."

"I've never known anything but soldiering, scouting, and sheriffing." Younkin knew how much the stable meant to Abe.

Were it not for his friend, he would not have stuck with it for as long as he had.

"You had the same eight years I had to change," Abe answered. "You didn't try. It was easier to tuck your tail between your legs and see the stable as a tombstone to your life."

"You've got it all wrong. You don't understand that—" Younkin tried to explain.

"To hell I don't! For the first time since you took off your badge, you were alive this morning." Abe stared at his friend as though seeing him from a different perspective. "I was so scared I almost dirtied my pants like some green private. But you loved it. The Comanches, the gunfire, it was like it used to be when we rode with Mackenzie. No thinking, no responsibility, just keeping yourself alive."

Abe's words struck close to home, but there was more to it. Younkin could not define it, could not vocalize the emotions that worked within him. He had tried to make the livery stable successful. It had not worked out. Things did not fit together the way they once did.

"Damned old fool." Abe spurred the roan toward the arroyo.

Bishop rose from a rock when he saw them approach. He waved them on. Younkin noticed a loose bandage flutter from the officer's left hand. Bishop called out, "Any sight of them?"

"Nothing." Younkin halted in front of the man and dismounted. "The hand?"

"Mostly blood. The bullet tore away the outer layer of skin. It will be all right." Bishop appeared twenty years older than when Younkin had met him two weeks ago. His face was drained and haggard with an ashen cast to the cheeks. His shoulders slumped forward, the military stiffness lost. "Ellis didn't make it."

Younkin's gaze followed the tilt of Bishop's head into the arroyo. Trooper Duncan Ellis's body lay beside his fellow soldier William O'Herne, who had died with a bullet between his eyes during the attack. Two men out of eight; Younkin tallied the losses. Black Hand had taken a heavy toll and suffered no losses. "What about Brooks and Compton?"

"The bullet went right through Brooks' right shoulder, sir." Michael Woebbe, the remaining uninjured trooper, approached. "I managed to get the slug out of Compton's leg. Bandaged both of them, and the bleeding seems to have stopped. They both said to thank you for the medicinal whiskey."

"Both men require a physician's attention," Bishop added.

"Can they ride?" Younkin asked Woebbe.

"If it's slow and easy . . . and not too far." The soldier glanced over his shoulder to his wounded companions, who rested in the shade. "If they reopen those wounds, they won't last long. Both men have lost a lot of blood."

"Can they make twenty-five miles?" Younkin edged back the brim of his hat.

"If the going isn't too rough, I'd say they had a good chance," Woebbe replied after a moment's consideration.

"Tuttle's Station is about twenty-five miles north. It's not much of a town, but they have a doctor." Younkin turned to Bishop. "We could be there before sunset."

"Tie Ellis and O'Herne's bodies to their horses, Private Woebbe," Bishop ordered his last able-bodied man. "Then get Brooks and Compton in the saddle. We'll ride as soon as you're ready."

Woebbe took two horses from Younkin and led them toward the dead men. Abe followed the soldier to help with the task.

"Four men . . . One minute everything was so quiet . . ." Bishop's face was dazed and vacant as though he still did not comprehend what had happened. "I didn't realize . . ."

Younkin dug at a stone in the sand with the side of a boot. He wanted to say something, but there were no words to comfort a man who had gone through what Bishop had. "There's a telegraph in Tuttle's Station. You can wire Fort Sill. After Abe and I get you to town, we'll ride on to Haas."

Bishop nodded, then his head snapped up. "Ride on?"

"There's not enough of your men left to keep after Black Hand, Lieutenant," Younkin said.

"There's Woebbe and myself." Bishop's shoulders straightened. Determination returned to his face. "And there's Potter and yourself. That's four men."

"That's *only* four men." Younkin studied the young officer intently. "We had eight this morning."

"I'd go after Toohmah if I were alone. I don't know if you can understand this, but those men were in my command. I was responsible for their deaths. I–I–I–" Bishop paused to take a prolonged breath. "I'm not certain *I* understand. Things have changed. It's no longer an assignment given by my superiors. It's personal. To give up wouldn't be right. It will not be right until those four Indians are captured and returned to Fort Sill to be hanged."

Younkin grasped the young man's shoulder. The pressure of his fingers conveyed the sympathy and understanding he could not express in words, or even wanted to place into words. The attack had brought to life an inner turmoil Younkin had thought was dead and buried. Tracking down Black Hand had always been "personal" with him, he finally admitted to himself. An old enemy lived and was as deadly as he had ever been. Despite all the lies he had told himself, he had accepted the job as scout for one reason—to complete a task he had left unfinished twenty-eight years ago.

"There's a possibility we can get ahead of the band again." Younkin looked at Bishop. "It'll mean three days of hard riding, starting tonight after we get Brooks and Compton to a doctor. But with luck, we can manage it."

"Continue, Mister Younkin." A glimmer of hope sparked in Bishop's eyes.

"This is the caprock." Younkin squatted on his heels to draw a rough semicircle in the sand with a fingertip. "We're here, south of it."

Bishop lowered himself beside Younkin.

"Directly north is Tuttle's Station." Younkin poked a finger into the sand above their location. "Here, to the northeast, is Haas. And here, just off the caprock to the southeast of Haas, are three mesas that the Comanches used to camp among. If Black Hand does like I'm thinking he'll do, he'll head for these mesas. There's a spring that flows from the base of the center one."

"If Toohmah swings around the caprock, he'll have a longer distance to ride than we." Bishop nodded and smiled.

"The country's rougher too, which should slow him down some," Younkin added. "There's no guarantee Black Hand will make for these mesas . . . just a feeling."

"A feeling is more than we have at the present, Mister Younkin." Bishop studied the sand map.

"In Haas, we can get the men we need," Younkin said. "You've met my son Tom. The mesas are within his jurisdiction. We can convince him to raise a posse."

"I like it, Mister Younkin." Bishop stood and looked toward the arroyo. Woebbe and Abe had tied the bodies of the dead soldiers across the backs of two horses. "I believe it's time we started for Tuttle's Station."

CHAPTER 12

Toohmah squatted beside the trickle of muddy water. He closed his eyes and let imagined currents swirl about his body. The cool stream washed away the sweat and dust covering him. The aches and tension seeped from his muscles and floated downstream. He opened his mouth; wetness, cold and refreshing, flowed in to soothe his throat.

A twinge of pain in his right leg dissolved the seductive illusion in a rush of reality. The Comanche opened his eyes. Red sand, partially concealing rounded, rust-colored stones, surrounded him. No rain swelled the river. It lay dry, except for the feeble ribbon of water that sluggishly flowed down the center of the dried bed.

The needles in his leg bit deeper. Toohmah found the rent in his trousers halfway between hip and knees. With both hands, he tore the black fabric wider to reveal a two-inch welt running across his thigh. Dried blood, black and crusty, formed a scab over the swollen wound.

Dipping a hand into the water, the brave filled a cupped palm, placed it over the welt, and rubbed gingerly. He sucked sharply through his teeth. The water reawoke the burning, like a firebrand pressed against his flesh. The pulsing waves of pain gradually subsided to throbbing needlepoints again.

The old *Nermernuh* examined the wound. His hand returned to the water three more times before the welt washed free of blood and dirt. He smiled sadly. The pain was another reminder of his age. While swollen and angry-looking, the welt was but a minor injury. The soldier's bullet had only grazed his flesh, peeling away the outer layer of skin the way a child does when he scrapes a knee.

Bathing the thigh twice more, Toohmah rose. His strides were strong and steady, without the slightest hint of a limp, when he joined his three companions who lay stretched on the ground near the river's bank. Ignoring the needles in his thigh, he lowered himself cross-legged to the dry grass and sand.

His gaze drifted over their faces. After six hours, fear dwelled in their young features. The corners of their mouths were drawn taut, their eyes darted nervously about, heads jerked anxiously when a jackrabbit bounded from a clump of mesquite.

Sadness suffused the old warrior's chest. He remembered another young brave and his first clash with the blue-coated soldiers. He recalled the taste of his own fear. The bitterness had faded only when he rode into the camp of the *Quahadi* band to be greeted by the proud cheers of his people.

There would be no such welcoming for these three, no joyous recounting of their bravery and deeds. That they still lived and rode free was all the reward they would receive for the courage displayed in the arroyo. It was not enough. They were cheated of the honors due braves returned from facing their enemies.

Toohmah lay back, shielding his eyes from the noon sun with the back of a hand. The sun's warmth eased the dissatisfaction from his mind. Twenty-seven winters weathered within the security of a tipi on the reservation had dulled his memory. He had forgotten how the cold sliced into a man's flesh to touch the bone and freeze the marrow within, forgotten how the wind blew across the prairie and lashed a man's face like an invisible whip intent on flaying the skin.

This second day of false spring pleased him, comforted his aged body with its warmth. It would not last, he realized. The weather was a coy promise of what awaited those who survived the winter. When the false spring ended, and it would tomorrow, the next day, or a week from now, the winter would rage, stronger and harsher, as though punishing the land for the sampled taste of luxury. The longer the unseasonable warmth lasted, the more severe would be the cold.

With fortune, we will be headed south by then, Toohmah thought. He would lead the small band north for four days. If no soldiers were sighted, he then would ride atop the caprock. There he would share the tobacco he carried in his saddlebags with the Sun Father and the Moon Mother. Afterward, he would ride to Mexico, away from the *Tejanos* and the soldiers. *With fortune.*

He rolled to a side to relieve the throbbing in his leg. It did not help. The needles persisted, jabbing hotly in his thigh.

Fortune walked with him, the *Nermernuh* assured himself. That morning when he faced the soldiers' rifles, he had heeded the *nenuhpee* warning. He had not killed. While Quinne, Chana, and Boisa Pah fired at the soldiers, his rifle barrel had been aimed above the Whites' heads. The explosions of his bullets added to the confusion of their escape, but he had not killed. Fortune would remain with him and the band.

A self-pleased smile uplifted the corners of the old brave's wrinkled mouth. In the face of disaster, good had prevailed. All four of them had come away from the arroyo alive and without injury to their ponies. Though his thigh ached, the wound was small. It would heal quickly, leaving a white scar to remind him of a morning when he had felt death's breath.

Toohmah pushed to his elbows. His companions had not moved. They neither spoke nor looked at one another. "We should eat while the horses rest." He hoped the remnants of fear would pass if they remembered their empty stomachs.

As the younger men sat up, Toohmah stood and walked to his bay. From the bottom of a saddlebag stuffed with unopened cartridge boxes, he withdrew a bundle wrapped in brown paper. He then took the canteens from the horns of each saddle.

He tossed the canteens to his companions, then unwrapped the brown paper and passed each a black twist of jerked beef, the last of the supply stolen from a rancher's smokehouse.

"Drink deeply, then fill your canteens from the stream. We will not find open water for four days."

Lowering himself to the ground, Toohmah gnawed a bite from the dry, smoked, and salted beef. He worked the meat between his teeth several minutes before it was soft enough to swallow. The jerky was a far cry from the pemmican he once carried in his parfleche. Even now he could taste the sweet mixture of dried buffalo, tallow, pecans, honey, and ground grain. He took another bite of the twist and chewed with determination.

"Uncle, will we now ride south to Mexico?" Quinne spoke around a mouthful of jerky.

Toohmah continued to chew, his eyes avoiding the gaze of the son of his sister's daughter.

"The soldiers can not be far behind us." Chana scratched at the splint bindings still tied around his left arm. "Can we lose them again?"

Toohmah swallowed and washed the beef from his throat with a swig of water. "I ride north when my horse is rested."

"The soldiers"—Quinne stared at his uncle in dismay—"know we are here."

"Yes, old man," Boisa Pah spoke. "What do you intend to do about the soldiers?"

"I do not fear the soldiers." Toohmah gnawed another bite from the twist. "They will not find us."

"They found us in the arroyo where you promised safety." Boisa Pah's tone seeped with contempt. "The Whites read your mind. Will you lead us north into their hands once more?"

"They will not find us," the old brave repeated.

"Easy for one who will not fight to say." The lanky warrior's voice rose, anger hardening it to an edge. "You have lost your craftiness, old man. You are a coward who is too afraid to even defend himself."

"My vision," Toohmah answered calmly. "I will not kill."

"Old fool! You sicken us with talk of your vision. You hide behind it like a child cowering behind his mother when he is threatened by his playmates." Boisa Pah hammered a fist against the ground. "You will lead us straight into the guns of the Whites. I will not die for a coward's vision!"

"You have not died, nor do you wear the soldiers' chains." Toohmah's eyes rolled up to the tall brave, challenging him.

"Mexico, old man." Boisa Pah pushed up so that he sat on his heels. Color drained from his coppery face. "You will lead us to Mexico, now!"

"I ride north—" Toohmah did not have time to finish. Boisa Pah, like a mountain lion uncoiling its powerful length, sprang.

The old Comanche's brain registered the action, but his body was too slow to react. He began a roll to the side when the younger man's full weight slammed into his stomach. Air driven from his lungs, nausea welling in his belly, Toohmah fell under the impact. Rocks bit into his back as Boisa Pah straddled him.

"Mexico, old man, or you'll end your journey here." The threat twisted its way through the younger brave's clenched teeth.

Toohmah gulped. No air came. A hand clamped around his throat and crushed inward. His arms wrenched upward, but did not move. Boisa Pah held them pinned to the ground beneath his knees.

"Mexico," the man above him demanded. "You will lead us to Mexico."

Boisa Pah's free fist arched high and fell, cracking sharply against the old man's chin. Toohmah's head snapped back. Pain lanced through jaw and neck. He twisted and bucked beneath the young brave, trying to unseat him. Boisa Pah's fist fell again.

Abruptly, Toohmah's throat was free, the weight gone from his chest. He struggled to his elbows and peered through the cloud of pain that fogged his vision.

Quinne and Chana wrestled with their companion. Boisa Pah raged like a man lost in bloodlust. His lanky body squirmed and jerked from beneath the hands and arms that sought to confine him. His fists pounded his companions, striking home on arms, legs, chests, and backs.

For an instant, he shook free of the two, defiantly glaring at them. To the old Comanche's surprise, Chana rushed his friend, his good arm flung wide to grasp Boisa Pah's waist.

Standing his ground until the last moment, Boisa Pah sidestepped the tackle. His right fist rose and fell like a hammer to slam into the back of Chana's neck. The pig-faced brave grunted and dropped to the ground. He lay there unmoving, dead or unconscious.

For an instant, Quinne froze, gaze riveted to Chana's still body. The hesitation was all Boisa Pah required. His hand dropped to the sheath strapped to his hip. The silvery blade came free and flashed upward, intent on opening Quinne's stomach.

As though just sensing his danger, Quinne leaped back. His left arm flew up to shield him from the knife. The blade bit, slashing a red line across the young brave's forearm. Quinne stumbled away from his assailant, right hand attempting to staunch the crimson flow.

Boisa Pah pivoted to face Toohmah. "Mexico, old man, or I swear you will not live another heartbeat."

Toohmah scrambled to his feet. His hand moved to his own hunting knife, then wrenched away as though he had touched a burning coal. The *nenuhpee* warning echoed within his head. Wildly, his eyes darted about him in search of a rock, a piece of wood, anything with which to defend himself. There was nothing.

Boisa Pah came at him, eyes wild, nostrils flared, a bestial growl rising from his throat. His blade lashed out in a wide arc.

The older man ducked. Naked steel hissed harmlessly above his head. Immediately, Toohmah sprang forward, moving inside his opponent's guard. His fist slammed inward to connect solidly with Boisa Pah's solar plexus. The younger brave groaned and doubled over. Toohmah's knee jerked up, driving into the man's nose. Boisa Pah reeled back. His arms flew out frenetically to fend off the unexpected assault.

Toohmah saw the flash of the blade but could not force his aged muscles to move fast enough. The knife nicked at his shoulder, opening his dark shirt and slicing into the flesh beneath. Something warm and wet trickled down the old man's chest.

Boisa Pah shook his head to clear it, then saw the trace of red that stained the tip of his knife. A broad grin split his angular face when his gaze returned to Toohmah.

"Now, old man, I'll cut out your heart and feed it to the buzzards!" Boisa Pah sprang forward.

Toohmah's hand dropped to his hunting knife. This time the blade slid free of its sheath. As the younger man slashed, he sidestepped and drew the knife's keen edge across Boisa Pah's cheek.

The lanky brave howled. His free hand slapped his face, fingers coming away red with blood. Madness blazed in the young man's eyes.

The cut was intended to awaken Boisa Pah to the danger he faced, to bring him to his senses. Its effects were the opposite. Boisa Pah lunged again, a war cry tearing from his throat.

Easily Toohmah defended the attack and lightly ran his blade across the back of his assailant's hand. Another crimson line opened on the younger man's flesh. Undeterred, the tall warrior came. Again and again, Toohmah danced away from the tip of his knife, a dangerous dance that could end his life with one misplaced foot. There was little else he could do; his vision could not be broken.

In a sudden change of tactics, Boisa Pah charged like an enraged bull. His knife, held low, swung upward in a blow meant to drive into the old man's stomach.

Toohmah stood his ground for a heartbeat, then threw out his right arm to deflect the attack. Fleshy weight slammed into his right hand. His knife was wrenched from his grasp.

Boisa Pah staggered back, eyes wide in bewilderment. His face twisted in an unspoken question. Slowly, he lifted his right arm and stared at his armpit. The pommel of Toohmah's knife jutted from the vulnerable flesh. Blood flowed around the dark handle.

Had Boisa Pah seen his defense and veered away at the last moment? Had his own reaction time been too slow? Toohmah did not know. It did not matter. His blade had driven home, burying itself where a man is the most vulnerable to a knife attack. No medicine man, red or white, possessed the power to mend the damage.

Boisa Pah dropped his knife and yanked Toohmah's from under his arm. The action only hastened the inevitable. Blood spurted from severed veins and arteries.

Without comprehension, the young brave looked at the older man. Gradually, Boisa Pah sank to his knees. He knelt motionless for a long, silent moment, then collapsed face down in the sand . . . dead.

The horror of the moment could not be denied. Anguish tore up from Toohmah's chest in a wailing cry. From the corner of an eye, he saw Chana rubbing his head, and Quinne, still clutching his arm, step toward him. He swirled on them. They stopped in midstride.

"My own people . . ." The words came like the cry of a rabid coyote. "One of my own people!"

Madness seared within his breast, sending dark tentacles upward to engulf his brain. One of his own people! His hands tore at the white man's clothes he wore, ripping them from his body. He stood naked, except for the breechclout he wore beneath. One of his own people! The vision was shattered. The *nenuhpee* would deny him . . .

"Noooooo!" The single word twisted from his lips.

Toohmah swirled and raced toward his mount. He found his rifle and wrenched it from its saddle holster.

"I have this!" He glared at Chana and Quinne. "I will not be denied what is mine. I will ride the plains of my people again. I will. Those who oppose me will die!"

Quinne and Chana stood mutely. Their gaze moved to Boisa Pah's body, then back to the old *Nermernuh*.

Toohmah's head lifted to the sky. He screamed the madness that consumed him into the face of the Sun Father.

CHAPTER 13

February 1, 1904

Jess Younkin reined the buckskin to an abrupt halt as he entered Haas's Main Street. Perplexed, he edged back the brim of his hat and stared at the mob of men crowded before the sheriff's office. "What the hell?"

"Haven't seen anything like this since Gerald Simpson tried to lynch that medicine-show professor in ninety-two." Abe drew his roan up beside Younkin. The black's forehead wrinkled with concern. "Must be every man in town."

And those from surrounding ranches, Younkin thought when he recognized several cowhands who normally made their way into town only on Saturday nights. "We'd best see what's going on."

"*You* see." Abe shook his head. "That many men make me nervous. I'll see to the horses and get us fresh mounts."

Younkin smiled at his friend's reluctancy and nodded. Swinging down from the saddle, he handed Abe the buckskin's reins. As Abe moved toward the livery stable, Younkin walked to the crowd and pushed his way toward the sheriff's office. He greeted the men who noticed him, repressing the frown that tried to crease his forehead. All the men were armed. Pistols were tucked in belts or holsters strapped about the waist. Each man carried a rifle or a shotgun. Younkin bit at his lower lip doubtfully. Haas's annual Thanksgiving Day turkey shoot never produced a turnout of men and firearms to equal what surrounded him now.

He reached the office and tried the door. The knob refused

to budge in his hand; the door was locked. Calling out his name to those inside, he pounded a fist on the door. Frank Galvin appeared at the office window and glanced at Younkin. A moment later, the door swung inward. Younkin entered and the deputy relocked the door behind him. Galvin offered no explanation when he noticed the older man's questioning expression.

"What the hell is going on here?" Younkin found Bishop and his son seated at the office's desk. The two looked up and smiled.

"Are they out there, Pa?" Tom asked.

"Depends on what 'they' you're talking about." Younkin walked to the desk. "Black Hand or that mob outside?"

"Black Hand," Bishop answered, motioning Younkin to an empty chair.

"They rode in this morning, and made a cold camp at the base of the middle mesa near the spring. From the looks of their horses, they've been riding at night and camping during the day." Younkin pulled off his hat and gloves and sank into the chair. "Now, will someone tell–"

"Perfect," Bishop interrupted before he could finish his question. "When Mister Milan and the other gentlemen arrive, we can begin."

"Dixon Milan? What's a merchant . . ." Younkin stopped. The rumbling of horseless carriages came from outside. Glancing at the window, Younkin saw the proprietor of the town's feed and seed, dressed in a white dust coat and goggles, driving at the head of a procession of Haas's ten motorized vehicles. The parade of belching machines halted before the sheriff's office. Younkin's head jerked around to his son. "Tom, would you mind telling me what's going on here?"

"Unbelievable, isn't it?" Tom grinned widely. "Renews one's faith in his fellow man. Each man out there has volunteered for the posse. Fifty men in all."

"This time we'll have the numbers needed to capture Black Hand," Bishop added. "Those four murderers will not escape us today."

"Three, Black Hand and two braves. There's only three at

the mesas." Younkin looked back at the horseless carriages. "What's Dixon Milan and the others doing here with those contraptions?"

"Three?" Bishop pushed to the edge of his seat. For an instant a perplexed frown hung on his face, then dissolved. "My men must have seriously injured one of them when they attacked at the arroyo."

"Perhaps." Younkin shrugged. "No way of telling. One of them might have decided to split from the rest. Comanche braves have always acted on their own. Comanches aren't like other Indians. They've never had a chief or any tribal leader, just braves banded together when it suits them."

Tom rose. "Frank, you and Hank tell the boys outside to load up. If we get moving, we can be at the mesas a little after noon."

"Load up?" It all fell into place within Younkin's mind. "You aren't seriously thinking about taking men off the caprock in those?" He jabbed a finger toward the window and the machines beyond.

"Dixon volunteered the use of his Oldsmobile and organized the others." Tom nodded, his grin growing with pride. "I read where a detective in New York City is using—"

"Damn! This isn't New York City!" Younkin stared at his son with disgust. "This is West Texas. It's fifteen miles over rough terrain to the mesas. Taking for granted those machines can make it that far, it's still no good. Black Hand will hear them coming before they're halfway there!"

"We've considered that possibility, Mister Younkin," Bishop answered in a condescending tone. "We believe the number of our men will compensate for the lack of the element of surprise."

"That's another thing." Younkin could not believe the stupidity confronting him. "We don't need fifty men. Fifteen men at most should—"

"I underestimated Toohmah once. I will not do it again." Bishop shoved from his chair. "If more men had volunteered, I would have accepted their help. The larger the posse, the better."

"Posse? That isn't a posse. That's a circus out there." Younkin glared up at the lieutenant. "Those men don't care about taking Black Hand alive. Every one of them is itching to kill himself an Indian. They're looking for a souvenir—a scalp they can hold up and brag about."

"Pa, you're making things worse than they are." Tom selected a rifle from a rack hung on the wall beside the desk and began loading it. "Those men have heard about Black Hand and the things he and his braves have done the past couple of months. Each of those men just wants to do his share to help keep the law."

"His share to keep the law?" Younkin shook his head sadly. "And they're going to do it with a circus on wheels?"

"It's a new century, Pa. You can't stand in the way of progress." Tom pulled on his hat and walked to the door.

"Maybe not." Younkin mentally conceded, realizing there was no way to convince his son of the folly of his actions. "However, I don't intend to sit beside Dixon Milan in that contraption of his."

"Have it your way," Tom said impatiently while he walked outside.

Younkin followed Bishop out of the office and stood watching while his son, the lieutenant, and their posse climbed aboard the waiting vehicles.

"Progress," Younkin mumbled under his breath. The horseless carriages rumbled to life and trundled down Main Street in a tight caravan. Cursing to himself, he started toward Abe, who waited in front of the stable with fresh horses.

Bishop lowered the binoculars to look up at Younkin, who rode beside Milan's Oldsmobile. "I don't see a trace of them."

"Not surprising." Younkin tilted his head to the cloud of dust that choked the air behind the column of automobiles. "Black Hand saw us coming an hour ago."

Bishop ignored the comment and peered through the binoculars again. Younkin shook his head and scanned the three mesas. The table-topped mountains jutted from the prairie in a tight triangle. At the apex rose the middle one, a spring trickling from its base. A quarter of a mile separated the bases of the mountains.

Nothing moved along the gentle slopes of the mesas. Odds were the three braves had fled when they noticed the vehicles' approach. The thought did not remove the niggling doubt that worried the scout as the column of automobiles moved between the two closer mountains. That one could not see a Comanche was not proof he was not there. The mesas' sides contained enough boulders and brush to hide men and horses.

"We'll proceed to the spring," Bishop shouted over the engine's deafening rumble. "Then we'll circle the mesa and see if we can pick up their trail."

Younkin nodded as he swung his mount to the right, rejoining Abe, who rode fifty yards to the side of the horseless carriages like an outrider on a trail drive. Younkin had resigned himself to the fact that any criticism he offered to Bishop would be shrugged off. The lieutenant, who had stood at the arroyo defeated and confused, now retreated back into the familiar security of military thought. That military logic did not fit the situation was of no consequence to Bishop, and there was no way Younkin could convince the man of his mistake.

An engine backfired.

The bay Younkin rode shied from the sound, lunging wildly to the side. Younkin gripped the reins firmly and wheeled the young horse around to face the source of the sound. Again an explosive pop rose over the din of the automobiles.

The second vehicle in the line swerved erratically. Charlie Shaw, Haas's mayor, lay slumped over the steering wheel of his Stevens-Duryea. The man beside him struggled to shove Shaw's limp body away and wrestle control of the wheel. The automobile's front tires turned sharply, biting into the sandy soil. The black-lacquered motorcar shuddered, its left side rising into the air. It teetered, balanced in midair on two wheels. Its occupants scrambled, leaped, trying to free themselves from the machine. Then it fell, rolling heavily to its back, wheels spinning uselessly at the sky.

"Gunfire!" Younkin shouted in warning. The popping cracks of firing rifles answered him. The bay reared, then bolted forward. Younkin yanked on the reins, halting the animal's flight before it began.

The neat column of horseless carriages broke into a ragged line. Each driver had seen what had happened to Charlie Shaw and now sought nonexistent cover.

"Circle 'em," Younkin called out. "Circle 'em."

Dixon Milan in the lead automobile tried to comply. He wrenched at the steering wheel to his Oldsmobile. In the next instant, Milan's vehicle joined Shaw's, tumbled upside down in the sand. Its passengers lay scattered on the ground about the overturned motorcar, except for Milan. Trapped behind the wheel, the proprietor of the feed and seed store had been crushed to death beneath the machine.

"They've got us in a crossfire!" Abe shouted at Younkin's side. He yanked his rifle from its saddle holster. "They're hidden in the rocks on all three mesas!"

Something hot and angry whizzed by Younkin's ear. Abe's mount reared high, too high. The black man kicked free of the stirrups and jumped from the saddle. He hit the ground rolling. The horse toppled to its back. Its legs kicked spasmodically, then went flaccid. A bloody hole existed where there had once been a right eye, marking the bullet's entrance to the animal's brain.

Rifle still in hand, Abe scrambled on all fours and dropped behind the dead horse. Another bullet sang by Younkin's head. Without hesitation, he swung from his mount and joined his friend.

"Like shooting fish in a barrel!" Abe said through clenched teeth. He cocked his rifle and squeezed off a round. "Damn!"

Younkin glanced at the confused scurry of automobiles. Billy Watters roared by in a green-enameled Knox. Watters and his passengers crouched low in the vehicle, attempting to make themselves as small targets as possible. They crouched too low. Watters did not see the narrow gully that ran in front of the vehicle. The Knox abruptly nosed into the gulch and disappeared. Flames belched into the air, chorused by screams.

"Damn!" Abe fired another shot. "They're out of range. They got the elevation on us. Even a rifle is useless."

As though to prove Abe correct, Younkin saw a man cut down as he jumped from a stopped motorcar. His companions leaped from the automobile and scurried beneath it. Their rifles returned the fire. Wisps of dust rose where their shots fell, a hundred feet short of their target, who crouched safely hidden amid boulders and mesquite.

The crunching crash of metal and glass drew Younkin's attention to his right. Two automobiles, in their drivers' panic, had collided. Smoke and steam billowed from beneath their rumbled hoods. Beyond the wreck lay two more overturned motorcars. The remainder of the motorized fleet had stopped. Their occupants either hid behind their bulk or lay under them for protection.

Volley after volley, the men emptied their rifles, reloaded, and emptied them again. The action was to no avail. The barrage was a waste of ammunition. Every shot fell short of its target. Eventually, the uselessness of their position becoming apparent, the men ceased the return.

A heavy silence settled between the three mesas.

Abe poked his head above the dead horse's side. "They stopped firing."

Younkin lifted his head to peer at the mountains. Nothing moved. Slowly he climbed to his feet. The silence remained.

"Get the hell back down here!" Abe tugged at his pants leg. "You trying to get your head shot off?"

"It's over." Younkin searched the rocky slopes. "They're gone."

"You crazy?" Abe stared up at his friend. "There's no reason for them to leave. They could pick us off one at a time."

"No reason for them to stay. Black Hand hurt us bad. That's all he needed to do. Delay us so he could ride on. Killing isn't what he's after. It's something else. We just happened to be in his way." Younkin turned to face the battlefield of smoldering machines and injured men. He grimaced, the full extent of the ambush's havoc apparent for the first time.

He reached down and helped Abe to his feet. "Come on. We've work to do in getting these men back to town."

"Three of the automobiles still run." Tom Younkin walked to where his father sat in the sand wrapping a wet cactus poltice around Billy Watters' burned arm.

"Injuries?" Younkin tied the makeshift bandage loosely about the arm. Watters winced and groaned despite his care.

"Fifteen bad, ranging from broken legs to gunshot wounds," Tom replied.

"Not all of them Black Hand and his braves' doing, I'd wager." Younkin helped Watters to his feet. "Dead?"

"Five, including Frank Galvin. A motorcar overturned on him." Tom hesitated, his eyes searching his father's face. "Pa, I didn't think it would be like this. I—"

"You didn't think." Younkin made no attempt to soften the harshness of his words. "If you're going to keep that badge on your chest, it's about time you started thinking."

Tom's mouth opened, but no words came forth.

"I've ordered the wounded who can't walk into the vehicles that still function." Bishop approached the father and son. "The rest of us will have to walk back to Haas."

"The rest of *you* can walk. I've still got a horse." Younkin motioned to the bay that stood nearby. "I intend to ride north after Black Hand."

"Back in town, we can outfit the posse with horses. Then we can . . ." Bishop began.

"You can shoot your thens and cans to hell!" Anger twisted knots in Younkin's chest. "Twice now, we've had Black Hand. And twice you've allowed him to escape because you wouldn't trust an old man's judgment. I can lead you to him again, but I'm not—that is, if you don't intend to listen to what I say. There's been too many killed. I don't want it to happen again, not without good cause."

Bishop stiffened, then went slack. He glanced at the ground. "Agreed, Mister Younkin. This time I'll follow your advice."

"Good." Younkin nodded his acceptance. "I want a total of

eight men, packed light and ready to ride hard. Unless I'm misjudging Black Hand, he and his bucks are headed north to Palo Duro Canyon. There's no way to beat him there, but we sure as hell can be on his heels."

"With Private Woebbe, Potter, you, and myself, we'll need four additional men," Bishop said. "And, of course, horses."

"Pa, Hank Wells and I would like to ride with you." Tom looked questioningly at his father.

Younkin considered mentioning that Black Hand was now beyond his son's jurisdiction, but let it pass. "You're welcome as long as you accept the terms I've laid out for the lieutenant."

"Accepted," his son answered.

"I'll leave it to you to pick the other two men riding with us." Younkin glanced at the bay. "Now I've some riding of my own to do."

"What about horses for us?" Bishop asked.

"That's what I'm going after." Younkin turned to Tom. "Your Aunt Jennifer's ranch is about ten miles northeast of here. I'll be back as soon as I can." He looked at Bishop. "The Army will, of course, pick up the bill on the horses."

Not waiting for the officer's reply, Younkin started toward his horse. Abe walked to his side. "Say hello to Miss Jennifer for me, Jess. And tell Lily there's one old nigger stuck out in the middle of nowhere that could do with some of her home cooking."

"I'll do that, Abe." Younkin smiled at his friend. Abe's on-off-on-off romance with Jennifer Steele's maid had been a ten-year affair. "Meanwhile, you see to it these men don't manage to kill themselves before I get back."

CHAPTER 14

Younkin watched the ranch hand mount and ride from the Steele house toward the coming night that darkened the eastern sky. The delay was unexpected, but unavoidable. The haggling necessary to complete the purchase of the horses had taken longer than anticipated.

"I apologize again about the horses not being here at the main house. Wayne moved the whole operation to the east house last summer after he bought a pair of Morgans. Wanted to keep everything under his eye. Sometimes my son acts as though I'm already dead and this ranch is his." Jennifer Steele looked up at Younkin and winked. She laughed. "As you can see, I'm still alive. And I guarantee Warren will have your eight horses here by early morning."

"No problem, Jenny. I wouldn't have gotten far with them before I had to camp for the night anyway. I'd forgotten how hardheaded you are when it comes to trading horseflesh." The widow touched a familiar intimacy within Younkin. Jenny was so unlike Clara, yet there was no denying they had been sisters.

"Of course you've forgotten. It's been six months since you darkened my door." Again she laughed, then reached out and touched his arm. "Even if you are a brother-in-law who only stopped by to rob me of eight fine horses, it's good to see you again, Jess Younkin."

"Miss Jennifer." Jenny's maid Lily opened the screen door and stepped onto the porch. She carried a pitcher of water and a bowl which she placed on a table set near the door. "Supper's ready. Like you ordered, Mister Jess's favorites, steak, potatoes and gravy, and pinto beans. For dessert, we've got canned peaches and pound cake." Lilly's ivory smile beamed at Younkin.

"Don't look like you're about to cut and run, Jess Younkin." Jenny's hands went to her slim hips. "It's not often I get company this far out. Since Wayne and Marion built the east house, supper's a lonely time. Wash up and come inside before everything gets cold."

"Only a crazy man would consider running away with a meal like that waiting for him." Younkin grinned while he washed arms and hands. He threw water on his face, noting a two-day stubble sprouted over his chin. "I could do with a shave."

"And a bath, I suspect." Jenny opened the door for him. "But you haven't heard anyone complaining."

They entered a hallway that led to a dining room that overwhelmed Younkin with its elegance. The darkly polished furniture, the imported mahogany paneling, and the delicate crystal chandelier that hung over a long, lace-covered dining table created the illusion that he had stepped into a mansion in Austin or Houston. The illusion was marred by the fact that the table legs sat within tin cans placed within larger cans. The larger containers held an inch's depth of kerosene, an admission of the harsh country surrounding the house. The kerosene kept ever-present crawling insects from finding their way up the table legs and into the meal.

"There's a grandness to this room and the lady it belongs to." Younkin seated himself at the head of the table at Jenny's urgings. The memories of numerous holiday parties Clara and he had attended at the Steele house crowded into his mind.

"The 'grandness' all belonged to Stephen." Jenny seated herself beside her guest. "He designed everything in this house. The 'grandness' lost its sparkle when he died two years ago. I don't believe a woman, except perhaps for my older sister, ever had a better man."

Younkin glanced up from the well-done steak Lilly had

placed before him. Physically, Jenny bore no resemblance to Clara. At fifty-five, Jenny was a smaller woman with bright blue eyes and sandy blond hair that only hinted here and there of gray.

Yet, in certain mannerisms such as the tilt of her head as she smiled, the gesturing hands when she spoke, the way a word rolled from her tongue, or the phrasing of a sentence, he detected the women's sisterhood. More than anything, Jenny, like Clara, had a way about her that allowed a man to relax and open himself. A man did not have to hide the feelings he carried from Jenny.

"It's hard with them gone, isn't it?" Younkin sensed the common loss they shared.

Jenny thoughtfully chewed a bite of steak as though pondering the question. "I don't know if it's any harder than it ever was. Or lonelier. Heaven knows this country is hard and lonely for a woman or a man on any terms. What I think is . . . well, it's less interesting. Every time I see Wayne and Marion's son Richard, I wish Stephen was here to see his grandson."

Jenny paused, her brow knitting while she sipped at her coffee. "Yes, I believe that's what I miss the most, the sharing. Never for the things that seem so important to us all the time. The sale of cattle, the mending of fences, the exchange of money from one hand to another: they always appear important, take up most a person's life. A man or a woman doesn't need someone else to help with that, except to pat them on the back occasionally or to complain to. But the small things, things we tend to overlook everyday, things that make up what a person really is inside, that's when I miss Stephen."

Her head turned to Younkin and she smiled. "Each day, even after two years, I see hundreds of things I want to show and share with Stephen. It's hard to put a finger on them. Perhaps it's a verse from the Bible I've just read, the awkward wobble of a calf when it first stands, a wild sow running through the brush with a line of piglets behind her . . . so many things."

She took another sip of coffee, and her gaze drifted about

the dining room. Were the memories as burdensome for her as for him? Younkin wondered while he studied her profile. The years had not diminished the beauty of the young girl he had first met at her sister's side in Austin twenty-nine years ago.

"Grandness," she smiled wistfully, almost to herself. "It wasn't always this grand. When Stephen and I settled here in seventy-five, we lived in a lean-to while Stephen dug a twelve-by-twelve room out of that little hill standing behind the house. That was our first home. Then, it seemed as grand as all this polished wood. All that mattered was that it was ours."

Younkin recalled the small house he had built for Clara after their wedding. It had been barely larger than the dugout Stephen and Jenny shared, but his and Clara's pride transformed it into a dream mansion.

"You know, the hardness of those times almost seems like pure enjoyment now." Younkin listened while Jenny reminisced about the small herd of longhorns Stephen gathered during their first years together. The herd grew, as did the profits when a market for Texas beef was discovered on the East Coast.

"Cattle, Stephen used to say, that was our life's blood. Said the land wasn't fit for anything but grazing cattle." Jenny shook her head. "Did you know Wayne farmed part of our acreage this year? Farming on the Steele Ranch?"

Younkin vaguely recalled hearing that Jenny's son had tried planting crops last spring. His head moved from side to side in answer, not wishing to stop the sound of his sister-in-law's voice.

"Cotton, grain sorghum, that's what he planted. Said it was the wave of the future for the caprock. Stephen would have tanned him good if he were still alive. Not that plowing the land had my approval, but one day all this will belong to Wayne, and he needs to start making decisions. I thought he'd come running to his momma when the crops failed, and I could say 'I told you so.' "

Nodding his approval, Younkin wiped the last trace of

gravy from his plate with a biscuit and popped it into his mouth.

"I was wrong, Jess." Jenny's chest expanded with pride. "Wayne even made a small profit off the crops. When it didn't rain, he tried something called irrigation, pumped water from one of the wells into the fields. Next year, he intends to plant more acreage."

"More and more farmers are breaking the land around Haas." Younkin drained his coffee cup. "When we first came to this country, we relied on mudholes, springs, and rain barrels for the water we needed. It's the windmills. They helped the ranchers, but they also brought the farmers. All a farmer needs to do is dig a well, and he's got water for his crops."

Noting Younkin's empty plate, Jenny called for Lily to serve dessert. When the black woman appeared from the kitchen, Younkin conveyed Abe's message. Lily grinned and assured him she would leave a meal for Abe wrapped in newspaper on the cutting board.

"Windmills, barbed wire . . . They brought the changes to this country, more than I thought I'd ever see." Jenny cut a bite of pound cake with a fork, but left it on her plate. "Maybe I'm doing the right thing, letting Wayne run the ranch. This country belongs to the young now. Some mornings I wake up feeling like I no longer know the world."

"Progress, that's what Tom calls it. He tells me the world changed with the new century." Younkin shook his head as he speared a peach slice. "Tells me my Texas is gone, part of the past."

He paused to swallow the last of his pound cake. "I don't know. I see the land around me, and it's the same as when Clara and I came to Haas . . . but the people are different."

"The land never changes, just the way men use it." Jenny reached out and gently touched the back of Younkin's hand. She smiled.

Younkin returned the smile, a bit chagrined. "Guess I'm sounding like an old man."

"Old men have the right to say their piece." Jenny's hand remained atop his.

"I reckon it's all changing too fast for me, Jenny. When we started to make our marks on the world, we knew what we wanted. We fought the Comanche for the land, then we fought the land and weather for a livelihood. Once all the fighting was through, the life we had planned never had a chance to get started. It was over before it ever began. I never noticed what happened or how." He leaned toward his hostess. "The world's not the one I imagined for myself. Farmers, trains, horseless carriages, they don't fit into the world we tried to build. Now the newspapers are telling about two men from Ohio who have built a flying machine. Sometimes I wonder if this is the same world I was born into."

"It seems confusing at times," Jenny agreed. "But I wonder if that's not the way it's always been. I suspect our parents and grandparents had visions of a world they wanted to build. I doubt if they passed on completely satisfied with what they saw. The trouble is, different men want different things. All those wants get jumbled together among one another. What finally occurs is something totally different than what anyone wanted."

"And the older you get, the less your wants and needs mean to anyone but yourself," Younkin concluded.

"Or maybe we keep trying to build that world that never had the chance to begin." Sympathetically, she squeezed his hand. Her blue eyes searched his face. "I believe Wayne left a box of cigars here the last time he came to visit. And I know there's a bottle of bourbon in the parlor. Can I interest you in either?"

"Both." Younkin grinned. "There's not a better way to top off such a feast . . . a good smoke, fine whiskey, and the companionship of a lovely lady to share them with."

A faint blush of pink touched Jenny's cheeks when they rose and moved into the parlor. After she seated him in an overstuffed chair by an open fireplace, Jenny poked a splinter of kindling into the flames to light a cigar, then passed it to him. He drew deeply, letting the blue smoke fill his lungs, then exhaled with pleasure while Jenny poured two fingers of Kentucky bourbon into two glasses. She gave one glass to

Younkin, then settled into another chair by the fire with the other. Normally, Younkin would have disapproved of a woman drinking strong spirits, but Stephen had never raised an eyebrow when his wife drank. Over the years, Younkin had grown accustomed to seeing Jenny sipping hard liquor.

"It surprised me that you never remarried after Clara's death." The fire's reflected flames danced in Jenny's eyes.

"Never seemed like there was time. When I gave up my badge, there was the stable." Younkin drank from his glass. It was the first drink he had taken in weeks. To his surprise, he discovered he really did not want it. The meal and Jenny's company were enough to satisfy him. "Besides, I doubt if any woman would have me."

"Now you're fishing for compliments, Jess Younkin," Jenny chided him and chuckled. "I'll wager you broke more than one woman's heart when you didn't start courting again."

Younkin sipped at the bourbon and smiled.

"You always did cut a handsome figure, Jess. I remember when you first came to my daddy's house in Austin." Jenny placed her glass on the floor and leaned toward the fire. "I was more than a little jealous of Clara. There was a time I used to pray you'd steal me away in the night and marry me."

Younkin's head snapped to the woman. He stared at her, uncertain he had heard correctly.

"Don't look at me like I'm some wicked Jezebel, Jess Younkin. We're too old and we've known each other too long to banter words about." Jenny's gaze met his defiantly. "Whether you'll admit it or not, you've always had an eye for me too. A woman can feel that, even if the man never says a thing."

"I'll admit it. You were a beautiful girl, Jenny." Younkin took a nervous swallow of bourbon. "You're still an eyeful for any man."

Jenny sank back into her chair, her eyes still locked on her guest. A pleased little smile moved over her lips. "Took you enough years to say that."

"A man doesn't go after his wife's sister." Younkin felt off balance by the turn of their conversation like some wet-behind-the-ears grammar-school boy. "Not if a man cares for his wife—no matter what he feels about the sister."

"Not that you'd have gotten anywhere. What Stephen and I had together was something special." That same smile remained at the corners of Jenny's mouth. "What I never understood was why you never came calling after Stephen's death."

"I guess I wasn't sure of how you felt." Younkin shook his head and downed the last of the bourbon. He waved an arm about the room. "No, that's not it. I thought about riding out here often enough. It was all this that stopped me . . . this ranch and the finery Stephen gave you, things I always wanted to give Clara. I could never give you what Stephen had. It didn't seem right for me to come calling."

"My fancy house, hmmmm." Irritation crept into Jenny's voice. "Do you believe this is all there is to me? My house and the fancy things in it?"

"No, but a man—" Younkin attempted to explain.

"A man lets his pride stand in the way of things that are important more often than not." Jenny rose from her chair and stood before Younkin. "Jess Younkin, come with me. There's something I want to show you."

Pushing from the soft cushions, Younkin followed the diminutive woman through the luxury of her home. Each room they passed through was less impressive than the preceding one as they walked toward the back of the house.

"Each room is a bit of history." Jenny glanced up at Younkin. "As Stephen got the money, he added a new room to our home. He never tore anything down. He said the rooms of the house were a living measure of how far we'd come in life."

Eventually, Jenny stopped in front of a plain, wooden plank wall near the back of the house. An equally unadorned door stood at the center of the wall.

"Wait here a moment. I'll get the lamp. What I want you to see is inside." Jenny touched his arm, questioning.

Younkin did as she requested, watching her disappear into the darkness beyond the door. He heard the striking of a match and the chiming clink of glass as she lifted and replaced the chimney of a lamp.

"Jess, you can come in now," she called to him.

He opened the door and stopped as he crossed the threshold, bewildered by what met his eyes. The room was small and cramped, no more than twelve by twelve. A feather bed, a chiffonier, and a dresser were crammed into the space. Worn wooden planks covered the floor, but the walls were dirt. The room was cool, and the effluvium of earth permeated the air.

"This is what Stephen and I originally began with, Jess. This is the dugout we lived in for three years." Jenny extended a hand to display the room. "Despite all the finery, we never stopped using it. More than any other room in the house, this is me. It's all I've ever wanted or needed."

Younkin's gaze moved about the cramped confines of the room. It radiated a strength that stemmed from the land out of which it was carved. Jess required no further explanation. He understood and shared something with her that exceeded his ability to define in words.

"I still use this room, Jess." She crossed the floor until she stood directly before him. The dimness of the kerosene lamp erased all traces of age from her face. For a moment, Younkin gazed upon the young beauty he had met in Austin half a lifetime ago. Jenny's lips trembled. "It's my bedroom . . ."

She paused. Her eyes darted from him to dance nervously about the room, then back to him. He saw uncertainty, doubt, within her gaze. She drew in a deep breath. "I'd like for you to spend the night here . . . in this room . . . with me."

She needed no other words. Younkin reached out and gently touched the softness of her cheek. The doubt faded from her blue eyes. His hands cradled her face. Awkwardly, he leaned down, his lips tenderly covering her small mouth as he securely enclosed her in his arms.

Younkin sopped the last of the egg yolk from his plate with a hot biscuit that dripped butter and honey. He closed his eyes and sighed with satisfaction as he savored the last bite of the breakfast. "A man could get fat and sassy if he was fed like this every meal."

"You could use some meat on your bones. You look a mite skinny to me." Jenny smiled at him across the kitchen table. She lifted a smoke-blackened pot. "More coffee?"

"A half-cup. Any more and I'll bust." Younkin held out his cup, enjoying the warm lethargy that suffused his body.

The sound of approaching horses came from outside the house. Jenny finished pouring the coffee, then rose to open the kitchen door. "It's Warren and the horses."

Younkin downed a hasty gulp of coffee, scalding his tongue and the roof of his mouth.

"Take it easy. It'll be a few minutes before he reaches the house." Jenny moved back to stand beside Younkin. Her hand rested on his shoulder. "I had forgotten how quickly a night can pass."

Younkin stood and slipped his arms around her slender waist. He tenderly hugged her to him and lightly kissed her lips. "What we had was good, Jenny. It was right. When I get back . . ."

"When you get back, I'll be waiting here for you." A blush of color reddened her cheeks. She smiled shyly and shook her head, a bit embarrassed. "I feel flustered. After last night, it seems kind of funny to feel this way . . . I can't let myself get shy now."

"Shy?" Younkin's eyebrows rose.

She glanced away from him. "I guess what I'm trying to do is propose to you, Jess Younkin, since I don't think you'll ever work up the courage to do it yourself."

Her eyes rolled up to study his face. "I want Wayne to take over the ranch, but this is a big spread. There's plenty here for two old people to make a life of their own on, to find a new purpose in living. Call it a dowry, but it's what I'm offering—it and myself."

Younkin's arms tightened about her. The awkwardness of last night had vanished. He kissed her, allowing all the new life he felt to flow from his body to hers. Reluctantly, their lips parted. "It's an offer I believe I'll take you up on . . . when I finish what I started with . . ."

"I understand." Jenny nodded, a smile of pleasure spreading over the beauty of her face. "I'll be expecting you, Jess Younkin. If you don't come back, I just might come looking for you."

The sound of the approaching horses grew closer. Their heads shifted to the kitchen door.

"I've got to finish this, Jenny." Younkin turned back to the woman who stepped from his arms.

"I know." Jenny reached out and took a newspaper wrapped bundle from the cutting board. "Don't forget this."

"Abe would never forgive me." He took the food Lily had prepared and walked outside with Jenny beside him.

"Take care of yourself, Jess. And remember, I'll be waiting for you." With a light kiss to his cheek, Jenny abruptly left him and reentered the house.

Younkin watched the door close behind her, then walked from the porch to greet the cowhand who approached.

CHAPTER 15

February 4, 1904

Chana discovered the calf two miles from the entrance to the canyon. Its head was firmly wedged between the trunks of two closely growing mesquite trees, apparently caught there while grazing. Abandoned by its mother and the rest of its herd when the young animal had been unable to extricate itself, the Hereford calf stood in the afternoon heat bellowing. It squirmed and twisted in panicked fear, its round eyes wide as the three Comanches approached. The desperate struggle was in vain. The calf's head remained solidly lodged in the natural death trap.

A single shaft sang from Toohmah's bow to end the calf's piteous cries and swiftly cheat nature of the slow, agonizing death by starvation it had decreed for the young creature.

Unwilling to delay long enough to properly dress the calf, Toohmah ordered Quinne to throw it over his saddle. The brave complied, and they continued northward, grateful for the fresh meat that would silence the hungry rumblings of their bellies.

A half-hour later brought the three within sight of the canyon. Its broad mouth opened for miles along the escarpment of the caprock. The two younger men turned to their aged leader and grinned, anticipating an end to their flight north.

Stirrings, warm and deep, awoke within Toohmah's breast. Fleeting glimpses of memories half forgotten with the passage of time flickered in rapid succession in his mind's eye. Within the confines of Palo Duro's high walls, generations of the *Nermernuh* had sheltered themselves from the ravages of winter's cold and icy winds.

The old Comanche nudged his horse forward, attempting to quell the rush of blurred images rooted in the past. Spiraling upward in that flowing stream wove a black twine like a poisonous serpent prepared to strike. Palo Duro Canyon was also a place of treachery.

There in the pre-dawn glow of morning, Mackenzie and his buffalo soldiers had accidently discovered the *Quahadi* band's hidden tipis. Like cowards devoid of the bravery enemies display when they face one another on the battlefield, the blue-coated soldiers attacked the sleeping camp. The raid ended in the slaughter of a vast herd of more than fourteen hundred Comanche ponies and mules, the true destruction of the *Nermernuh*. Hungry, shelterless, the People's feet had been placed on a long winter's path that eventually led to Fort Sill and the reservation.

Ghosts, like those that haunted the clearing along the Brazos River, awaited Toohmah within the canyon. He felt their presence pressing out from the yawning mouth of rock to greet him, ready to suck away his soul should he falter in his purpose.

There was no turning back now. He was too close to his goal. With or without the protection of the *nenuhpee* vision, Palo Duro offered him a passageway to the High Plains. Again, his bootless heels nudged his mount's flanks. The bay gelding broke into a trot. Behind the old brave, Quinne and Chana urged their horses after him.

The past and future melted to the present when the three reached the canyon's wide entrance. Toohmah halted and pointed to an abundance of hoofprints covering the sandy floor. The abandoned calf so near the canyon and now the prints indicated the presence of Whites.

Leery of what waited within, Toohmah clucked between his teeth to the bay. The horse moved ahead at its own cautious pace while its rider eyed the high walls that rose to each side of them.

"Are the Whites hiding in—" Toohmah raised a hand to silence Chana's question.

Again the old brave reined his horse to a halt. He slid from the saddle and walked a few strides to squat on his haunches. A moment later, he stood and turned back to his companions, a smile lifting the corners of his mouth.

"The most recent tracks lead from the canyon. Some *Tejano* cowherder has used Palo Duro to protect his cattle from the cold winds." Toohmah swung back into the saddle. "With the warm weather, he has taken the cattle from the refuge of these walls."

Eyes still watchful, Toohmah rode deeper into the immense abyss carved by eons of wind and water. If one white man utilized Palo Duro to protect his herd, others might be concealed by the two hundred and fifty miles of canyon that fed into what the Whites named the Prairie Dog Town Fork of the Red River.

A half-mile from the canyon's entrance, Toohmah led the younger men from the main gorge to follow a dried creek bed that emptied into the streamlike river. Fifty yards beyond the mouth to a minor canyon branch, he ordered the two to prepare a camp for the night.

While Quinne filled the canteens at the river, Toohmah carefully cut away the splint Chana had worn on his left arm for five weeks. Exploring the arm with probing fingers, Toohmah found no telltale knots on the bone that would indicate a bad set.

"The bone is like new," the old brave finally pronounced. "Strong enough to gather wood for a fire."

Grinning as he tested his arm with his right hand, Chana circled the area to gather dried branches of oak, mesquite, and cedar. Toohmah called Quinne to him. Unwrapping the young man's bandaged arm, he washed the wound left by Boisa Pah's blade. Portions of the five-inch gash remained raw but displayed no signs of festering.

"Clean it daily and it will heal, leaving only a thin white scar," Toohmah told the son of his sister's daughter. "Now help me with the calf."

Together, they pulled the carcass from Quinne's saddle and used their hunting knives to skin the red-and-white hide. Deftly, Toohmah worked his blade under the backstrap and cut away the choice portion of meat. He passed the bloody strip to Chana, who speared it with a makeshift wooden spit and held it over the growing flames of a small campfire.

Ten minutes later, Toohmah and Quinne finished dressing the remainder of the calf. The unprotected meat would spoil rapidly in the unseasonally warm weather. There was nothing they could do to stop the natural deterioration. However, it would be fresh enough to provide another meal in the morning and perhaps tomorrow night.

The angry hissing of hot grease dripping into the fire drew the two beside Chana and the cooking backstrap. Toohmah sat cross-legged in the sand beside the flames for a long silent moment. The aroma of the veal was overwhelming. Unable to endure his stomach's rumblings until the meat was thoroughly cooked, he waved for Chana to remove it from the flames. The young brave complied, slicing a portion of the sizzling beef for his companions, then one for himself.

Toohmah's teeth tore into the meat; juices and grease trickled from the corners of his mouth to glisten on his chin. He gulped down several mouthfuls of half-chewed beef, slowing when his belly's loud protests ceased.

Only then did his attention wander from the meal to his surroundings. He nodded silent approval. The campsite he had selected was good. The fire could not be seen from the main gorge, nor could their position. The narrow mouth of the tributary canyon would be easily defendable should Younkin and the soldiers still follow. One guard stationed among the boulders at the entrance could observe anyone who moved into Palo Duro.

His head tilted back to let his gaze climb the canyon's walls. Three-quarters of the way to the top, the wall was sloped in a gentle incline. Despite the sandy soil and loose rocks, a man could casually walk up most the wall. The last two hundred and fifty feet were the hardest, requiring a man to actually climb the face. However, it was an easy climb with many footholds and handholds. As a child, Toohmah had scaled the walls of the canyon in search of lizards and birds' eggs.

Atop the towering wall—the High Plains, the flat, prairie lands of the caprock. He smiled. His feet would tread that soil once more before he passed into the Valley of Ten Thousand-fold Longer and Wider. He had but to climb the wall to reach his destination. Not even his age would prevent that. It should take no more than an hour for him to scale the rocky face, such a short distance to overcome after the long, meandering flight from the reservation. He had not needed medicine to protect him, nor the aid of the *nenuhpee*. He would complete his journey. His own unfaltering determination was all he required, all he ever needed. He laughed aloud, feeling a weight lift from his shoulders.

Quinne and Chana, grease smeared over mouths and hands, looked up from their meal. Quizzical expressions furrowed their faces.

Toohmah grinned widely at his companions. "In a day, two at the most, we will begin our ride south to the Mexican border."

The younger men's faces remained unchanged. Toohmah laughed again. "There is a narrow trail up river that leads to the caprock. We can ride our horses up that trail. Once my feet have walked the High Plains, I will be ready to travel south."

Quinne and Chana's puzzled frowns transformed into broad grins of relief. It was the first happiness Toohmah had seen in their faces since they had faced the soldiers at the arroyo. Their joy increased the soaring of his own heart.

"We will camp here for the remainder of the day and night to rest ourselves and the horses. When we ride again, we will not rest until we have moved down the caprock to the south." Toohmah pointed to the top of the canyon. "The High Plains are open and offer no shelter to conceal a man. Our cloak will be the fact that the Whites will not expect us to ride so boldly through their land."

Toohmah tore another bite from his piece of backstrap. He

chewed twice, then laughed out loud once more. This time Quinne and Chana joined in his laughter. The sound echoed off the walls of the canyon and rolled back on them.

"Even the land shares our joy." Quinne reached for the spit and sliced another portion of veal.

Toohmah's head tilted to the entrance of the tributary canyon. "Who wishes to take the first watch?"

Quinne nodded, rose, and began to walk to the entrance. Toohmah watched him, feeling the pride of a father for a son. Young in years, Quinne was no longer a boy, but a man. Even in the days before the reservation, he would have ridden with the other braves of the band. None would have denied his manhood or his courage.

Reaching the mouth of the small canyon, Quinne positioned himself behind the talus and boulders that lay at the foot of the wall. Toohmah gave his unspoken approval. Quinne had learned much in the time that had passed since their escape. Were it necessary, he could lead Chana to Mexico.

Were it necessary. For an instant, the image of the *nenuhpoo* warrior and the double-edged blade he carried filled Toohmah's mind. *No!* He shook off the vision. There would be no need for Quinne to lead. Medicines and visions no longer held meaning for him. He would walk the caprock, then ride to the land of the *Mejanos.*

"The fire grows low." Toohmah motioned to the flames as Chana cut himself another slice of beef. "Place enough meat for two meals over the coals. We will carry it with us when we leave."

The younger man immediately began his task. The days of hard riding and little food had also transformed Chana, Toohmah noted. No longer did he deserve the name "hog." While he still shied from using his left arm, muscle, hard and solid, rippled along the length of his right while he lifted a leg from the dressed carcass and began to cut at it with his knife.

"We will have to find a name more suited for you than Chana," Toohmah announced. "It is not a name for a warrior to carry."

Chana smiled, but did not stop his work.

"Is there a name that pleases you?" Toohmah asked.

The leg came free, and Chana moved back to the fire. "I have never thought of being called by any other name."

"The People once considered it an honor to bestow a name upon a brave that reflected the greatness of his deeds." Toohmah pulled the last of the backstrap from the spit.

"Then I would be honored if you chose a name for me." Chana looked up and nodded solemnly at Toohmah.

"Such things should not be done hastily. I will think upon it." Toohmah stood and walked from the fire.

Twenty feet away, their three horses stood, reins wrapped about a mesquite tree. Untying them, Toohmah lead the mounts around a sharp bend two hundred strides farther down the canyon. Hobbling their front legs with strips of cloth cut from the white man's clothes he carried in his saddlebags, he removed their bridles and saddles.

Satisfied the horses could graze but were unable to wander far, Toohmah threw his saddlebags filled with cartridge boxes over a shoulder. He returned to Chana and stretched out on the ground by the fire. A breeze moved over his half-naked body. Moisture hung heavy in the air. Winter's false spring had lasted for weeks. It would change soon, bringing rain or, worse, ice and snow, with the change. He would once again have to don the white man's clothes. Until then, his breechclout and leggings sufficed.

His gaze wandered up the canyon's walls. He smiled to himself. No ghosts dwelled here, only memories. How many times as a child had he played among the rocks and sand here, or helped the band's older men gather fine cedar for bows and arrows? As a youth, he had hunted the antelope and rabbit that sought the canyon's shelter in winter. Here, he had courted and won the hand of a woman who bore him a son. Here, he had brought her father thirty ponies to pay for the young bride. And within the walls of Palo Duro they had first lain together as husband and wife, man and woman.

His attention focused on the canyon rim. The urge to climb the wall crept into him to grow like a cry that sprang from deep within the chest. His muscles tensed, ready to answer that call.

No; he shook away the reckless urge. Soon enough he would ride the trail leading upward to the caprock. Such a climb was foolishness. While he was certain he could scale the steep face, the risk was too great with his goal so close. If he were to fall, the *nenuhpee* vision would be proven true.

Toohmah closed his eyes to remove the temptation. The fragrance of nearby cedars coyly wafted into his nostrils. He basked in the warmth of the fire and the sun above him.

Here and now, it was so easy to imagine that time had stood still, that the reservation and the Whites did not exist. He was young once again and the *Quahadi* band lay camped but a few miles up the canyon. Soon he would return to his people with fresh meat for his tipi.

For years, he had not allowed himself the luxury of such mental wanderings. Now, Palo Duro gave them new life. They caressed and comforted him like the soft fingers of a woman. He nestled into their arms, succumbing to their seductive embrace. Backward through time, he allowed those gentle arms to carry him, until he stood at the center of the universe, one with himself and the land.

"Uncle." A hand shook Toohmah's shoulder, nudging him from a half-sleep. "Riders approach."

The old brave forced open his eyes. Quinne and Chana hovered over him, their faces filled with concern. Toohmah pushed to his elbows. "How many?"

"Seven or eight," Quinne answered. "They just entered the canyon."

"The fire, cover it." Toohmah pointed to the smoldering coals. As he gained his feet, Chana moved to the cooking meat and began scooping handfuls of sand onto the remnants of the campfire.

At Quinne's side, Toohmah trotted to the mouth of the tributary canyon and crouched behind the rocky cover. Cautiously, he peered over the boulders. Eight riders moved down the center of the main gorge.

"Soldiers?" Chana joined them, carrying three rifles. He handed each of his companions one.

"Two are soldiers." Silently Toohmah cursed. He had no doubt the scout Younkin had survived the ambush at the mesas and now led these men after them.

"What do we do now?" Chana peered over the boulders, then looked to Toohmah.

"Wait." The older man cocked his rifle. "There are many tracks on the canyon floor to confuse those left by our horses."

Toohmah heard the metallic clinks of the younger men's rifles as they followed his lead and cocked their weapons. With fortune, there would be no need for an attack. If the Whites did not notice their tracks, they could ride by the small canyon, searching for their prey deeper in Palo Duro.

The eight men rode closer. They talked among themselves, but Toohmah could not discern if they followed the fresh hoofprints left by their three horses. Mentally, the old Comanche offered a prayer to the gods who had abandoned him.

Chana caught his breath. The Whites stopped. One man swung from his mount and sank to a knee beside his horse in the sand.

"They have sighted our tracks," Chana whispered as he glanced to his companions.

No; Toohmah released an uneasy breath. The man only dismounted to examine the foreleg of the black mare he rode. The tracks had not been seen.

From the corner of an eye, the Comanche caught a blur of motion. Chana stood. The young man's rifle rose to his shoulder. Toohmah's arm shot out to jerk Chana back behind the boulders. Too late!

Chana's finger squeezed the trigger. The rifle's explosion echoed like thunder through the canyon. The man on his knees jerked into the air, flying backward and falling to the dirt. The man did not rise.

The remaining riders came alive. Jerking on their mounts' reins, they wheeled and rode hard for a rocky outcropping to their left.

The curse that rose in Toohmah's throat remained unspoken. He rose and fired, as did Quinne. Their action came too late. The Whites vanished behind the rocky shelter. Within the beating of a heart, the staccato barking of rifles returned the Comanches' fire.

Toohmah and his young companions dropped behind the boulders and talus once again. The whine of the Whites' bullets ricocheted harmlessly off the canyon wall.

In a silent plea, Toohmah's eyes drifted upward to the sky overhead. The canyon's rim drew his gaze. Only a thousand feet away, so close. A tremor ran through his body. He struggled away from the thought before it could find substance in his mind. Yet a shadow of its meaning remained, haunting him, leaving him with a fear that he would never scale those steep walls.

CHAPTER 16

The bitter taste of bile settled thickly atop the dryness of Younkin's mouth, threatening to choke his fear-constricted throat. Sweat trickled in rivulets from his brow despite the coolness of late afternoon. His temples reverberated with the thud-a-thud pounding that echoed up from his heart.

A bullet slammed into the canyon wall above him to ricochet off the rock with a hot and angry scream.

Younkin's head dropped to the ground; sand and dust coated the side of his face and clogged his nostrils. He clamped his eyes tightly closed as a shower of stone fragments cascaded from above to bite into his exposed cheek. Teeth clenched, he endured the needles of pain that probed under his skin.

A volley of rifle fire from the men behind him answered the single shot that had struck overhead.

Gathering himself, Younkin began to crawl once again. Sunk behind the cover of a low line of boulders and talus at the foot of the canyon wall opposite Black Hand's position, he inched his way forward. His hands reached out, dug into the sand, and pulled. His torso and legs squirmed after them.

Somewhere along the two hundred feet that separated him and his companions, who were concealed behind the relative security of the rocky outcropping, his sense of humanity had retreated to the recesses of his being. He was no longer a man, but a frightened creature that scuttled along with its belly sunk in the dust. Survival—to live to crawl the next few feet—dominated his existence.

He recognized the fear, had tasted it briefly nine days ago when he had crept along the arroyo south of the caprock. It was the same fear he had first encountered when only eighteen as he stared at a desperate charge of blue-coated Union soldiers. For forty-two years he had not conquered the fear, only lived with it.

Now, as with all the occasions on which the fear had raged inside him, he fought it with the only emotion he contained that equaled its intensity—hate. His arms stretched out, hands dug into the ground, and body wiggled after them. He crawled forward to destroy the thing that forced him to confront the weakness that dwelled within him.

Images of a butchered wife and child, the countless deaths of friends at Comanche hands, nursed the hate, provided a rationale for his actions. Beneath the convoluted logic his mind manufactured, the outward veneer, lay the fear and his shame of possessing such terror. The personification of that fear, the mirror that reflected its image, was an old Comanche named Black Hand. To kill him would erase the image from Younkin's mind.

Stomach dragging the ground, the man transformed to a terrified animal wriggled forward until he lay directly across from the Comanches' position. He unstrapped the Winchester about his shoulder and rolled to his back. Rifle balanced on chest, he cocked it. A sharp metallic click sounded as a cartridge was injected into the chamber.

Cautiously, he pulled upward, his head briefly poking above the foot-high barrier of rock that protected him. Immediately he dropped back; a curse spit from his lips.

His position offered no advantage. The boulders at the mouth of the tributary canyon provided a perfect fortification for the Comanches. To crawl farther would be useless. The western wall of the minor canyon would then block his line of fire.

Once again, he peered across to Black Hand's position. Nothing. As he lowered himself, he halted. A movement, deeper into the small canyon, caught his attention. He squinted, barely making out the exposed haunch of a horse and the flicking of its tail. A humorless smile moved over the scout's lips.

Dropping back behind the rocks, Younkin began to scramble back to his companions.

Tom Younkin and Lieutenant Bishop critically eyed the route Jess Younkin had successfully traversed. Eventually, their heads turned to Abe.

"Jess is right. If we can get to their horses, the three will be trapped. The plan's a good one." Abe nodded thoughtfully. "There's no way they'll try and climb the canyon with us sitting here. Black Hand knows we could pick them off easily. Even at night they wouldn't have much of a chance of going up the wall."

"There's no guarantee you'll find a place to scale the wall farther down the gorge," Tom protested, looking back down the course his father proposed to take.

"No, but it's worth a shot. Even if we don't, Abe and I can move in on them from the opposite side of the entrance. Force them farther into the canyon and hopefully into a less defendable position," Younkin answered.

"I still don't like it. You're both too . . ." Tom faltered.

"Too old?" Younkin shook his head and looked at his son. "Old enough to know better than to try and climb something steep enough to get us killed. Or try something as foolish as going after Comanches in horseless carriages."

Tom and Bishop winced at Younkin's last comment.

"The only thing you need to worry about is giving us heavy cover when we reach the end of those rocks," Younkin continued. "There's ten feet of open space before the western wall of the canyon mouth will hide us from Black Hand."

"The plan has my approval." Bishop looked at Abe, then at Younkin. "Whenever you're ready."

Younkin saw his son's mouth open. Before Tom could voice further objections, he turned and started to belly-crawl behind the low cover of scattered boulders and stone. Abe, rifle strapped over a shoulder, dropped to the sand and inched his way after his friend. Younkin glanced behind him to see the army officer and Tom take their positions with the other men.

Ten minutes later, Younkin reached the end of the natural barrier. He peered around the rocks, but still could not glimpse the Comanches hidden among the boulders at the mouth of the tributary canyon. He looked back at Abe. "Signal Bishop."

A barrage of heavy rifle fire pelted into the boulders concealing the three Indians in answer to Abe's wave. Younkin shoved from the sand to his feet. In a crouched run, he covered the open space, stopping when the entrance to the small canyon was out of sight. He turned and motioned to Abe.

Again the black man signaled Bishop. Another barrage of bullets tore into the Comanches' position. Abe rose and ran. Before the echo of the rifle fire died, he stood beside Younkin. His breath came in heavy heaves. "I'm too damn old for this foolishness."

"Nothing foolish about it." Younkin answered without humor. "Neither one of us drew a single shot. Black Hand and his bucks didn't see us."

Abe's lips puckered with disgust. Younkin ignored the expression and started deeper into Palo Duro. A hundred yards from the tributary canyon's entrance, he crossed the main gorge to the opposite wall. He considered edging back to the smaller canyon's mouth and taking the three Indians by surprise, then discarded the idea. Later, if his plan failed, it would be worth a try. Now, it was too reckless. No need to expose themselves unless it was absolutely necessary.

Pulling the Winchester from his shoulder, Younkin worked westward. His gaze constantly surveyed the canyon's formidable heights. They afforded no hope of an easy climb.

"This idea of yours is worth about as much as teats are on a boar hog," Abe muttered, head tilted back to the canyon's rim.

"Better than sitting on our tails and ducking bullets." Younkin stopped. He pointed down the canyon. "Take a look at that."

Abe followed his extended finger. A half-mile beyond them, the canyon's solid wall abruptly dropped to a mound of earth and rock rising no more than two hundred feet in a gentle incline. The two men trotted to the foot of the collapsed wall. Cautiously, they picked their way up the mound of sand and stone. Another canyon, smaller in its width, opened on the other side of the crumbled wall.

"No guarantee this leads to Black Hand." Abe turned to his friend. "Could be an eddy canyon."

"Could be a path to a secluded cathouse, but it isn't." Younkin started to descend into the smaller gorge. "We haven't seen another spur canyon. This is what we're looking for."

"Only one way to find out." Abe's boots slipped and slid in the loose sand.

Reaching the floor, the two followed a dry creek bed eastward. The report of rifle fire echoed louder with each step they took. Younkin smiled to himself. The Comanche never learned. As Mackenzie had done twenty-eight years ago, he would rob Black Hand of his horses. On foot, the Comanche was nothing but another jackrabbit running through the underbrush. He recalled the fear that had knotted his insides less than an hour ago and shook his head. A man feels strange, confusing things when he is faced with the unknown. Now there was no fear, only a feeling of elation, an anticipation of easy victory.

Ahead of them, the canyon took an abrupt bend. Younkin and Abe hugged close to the rocky wall as they approached the angular turn. Younkin's head slowly poked out beyond the wall's protection. A broad grin split his face.

"We've got them." Younkin pushed from the wall.

Abe stepped after him. "Damn, never expected it to be this easy."

Before them the canyon floor spread in a broad clearing covered in winter-dried grass. Three horses, necks bowed to the ground, stood peacefully grazing.

Younkin cocked his rifle, hefted it to his shoulder, and took a bead on the horse nearest him. His finger tightened around the trigger and squeezed. The black gelding lurched. His hobbled legs jerked, straining to break the binding that held them. The horse stiffened, then fell to the ground, a red blossom spreading from its left temple.

Abe's rifle answered the echo of his shot. A bay collapsed to its knees. It teetered there a moment before its back legs wrenched spasmodically and it rolled to its side, dead.

Younkin sighted on the third animal and pulled the trigger.

Two rifle shots resounded from the canyon walls.

"Damn!" Abe spun around, clutching his shoulder. He dropped to one knee, a pained expression contorting his dark face.

Another shot exploded. An angry swarm of wasps whizzed by Younkin's left ear. His head jerked to the dead horses. Beyond the butchered animals stood a lone brave, rifle raised to his shoulder. A barking crack exploded from the weapon's muzzle.

Younkin leaped toward Abe. He hit the ground in a head-over-heels roll that brought him back to his feet. His Winchester swung to the Indian and he fired, emptying the rifle as fast as he could cock cartridges into the chamber. The brave scrambled back to seek the wall's protection.

One arm hooked beneath Abe's left armpit, Younkin pulled his friend to his feet. In a lopsided gait, they made their way behind the sharp bend in the canyon, out of the brave's line of fire.

"God," Abe moaned; his hand clutched his shoulder. "It hurts. I've never felt anything hurt so much. I've got to rest a minute, Jess."

"One minute." Younkin dug spare cartridges from a pocket and reloaded the rifle. "Time's up."

"Jess, I can't . . ."

Younkin did not listen. He threw his friend's good arm over his shoulder and wrapped one of his own arms about Abe's waist. He dragged Abe with him in a half-run. He risked a glance behind them. The brave did not follow.

They reached the break in the canyon's wall. Stumbling and sliding in the loose soil, Younkin struggled up the mound, tugging Abe along with him. At the crest, he dropped to the other side and lay the injured man on the ground. Younkin raised his rifle and waited. The brave did not appear. Why hadn't he followed? It made no sense. He should be after them like coyotes after a stranded calf.

"It's bad, Jess." Abe's head rolled to his friend. "It feels worse than the one I took back in Tarrant County in seventy-two."

Younkin lowered the Winchester and dropped to his knees at Abe's side. His fingers worked open the buttons to his friend's shirt and pulled back the coarse flannel fabric.

Blood spouted from the wound in pulsing spurts: too much blood, far too much for a shoulder wound.

Tearing the shirt, Younkin pressed the cloth against the wound to staunch the crimson flow. The light-blue flannel deepened to a dark purple, then red. Blood saturated the fabric. Younkin ripped another piece of the shirt and pressed it atop the round hole. Firmly, he held it in place with an open palm.

"How is it?" Abe stared up in a pained grimace. "It hurts so damned much. I didn't know anything could feel as bad as this."

"It's not bad." Younkin lied. The bullet had torn something within the shoulder, an artery from the way the blood came in spurts. Moisture seeped from beneath the makeshift bandage. "I'll have the blood stopped in a minute or two. We'll have you back with the lieutenant in no time. Then Woebbe can patch you up."

"There ain't no all right about it, Jess. I can feel that." Abe's words came slow and slurred. His eyes rolled upward to the sky. "I feel so weak . . . like I'm bad sick . . . weak . . . sleepy."

"No time for sleeping." Younkin stuffed another piece of flannel beneath his hand and pressed down. "We've got to get you back to Woebbe."

Abe coughed. A trickle of red ran from a corner of his mouth. Had the bullet struck a lung as well? Panic gnawed at Younkin. There was nothing he could do for his friend.

"Sleepy." Abe's eyes fluttered closed.

"Don't go to sleep on me, Abe." Younkin shouted into the black man's face. "Think about Lily. Think about her chicken fried steak and pound cake."

"Steak . . . pound . . ." Abe's dark eyes opened to thin slits. A weak smile uplifted his mouth. "Lily . . . she's going to miss me, Jess. Damn, but . . . she's going to miss . . . me. Ain't . . . another nigger . . . within a hundred miles . . . of Haas. Should have married her . . . Jess."

"Ain't nobody going to miss . . ." Abe's body went flaccid. His eyes opened wide in an unseeing stare. Younkin gazed at his friend, knowing, but refusing to accept what had occurred. "Wake up you old fool. Wake up!"

He shook the limp body. Abe's eyes did not move. The smile had vanished from his face. No expression remained on those ebony features, only the lifeless mask of death.

"You old fool . . . you old fool . . ." Younkin gathered his friend in his arms and hugged him to his chest. "You can't go and die on me. You've got a livery stable to keep. You've got . . ."

The words, the self-deceiving lies, would not come. Pain constricted Younkin's throat; he gasped for air in shallow gulps. Tears welled from his eyes and streamed down his cheeks. A quaking tremor of realization shuddered through his body. "You can't leave me here . . . you can't leave . . ."

Something broke within the aged scout. Heaving sobs racked him. Unashamed of the feelings, the loss, he wept to release the flood of agony that ripped through his soul.

An hour, a day—Younkin had lost all sense of time when the violent shuddering finally passed and the tears no longer came. He stared about him, uncertain. Dusk veiled the mound, its hue deepening into night. Gently he lowered Abe's head to the ground and touched his cold, dark cheek.

A furtive memory, coy and elusive, hid itself within his mind. There was a reason for this, but it evaded him. There was something he had to do, something that needed to be completed . . . something . . .

Younkin picked up his rifle and stumbled to his feet. Dazed and uncertain why he stood here beside his dead friend, he walked to the mound's crest. He hesitated, unable to orient himself, then started downward in a half-slide, half-walk.

The ground abruptly leveled under Younkin's boots when he reached the floor of the tributary canyon. He stopped, neck craning back while he searched the mound behind him. The darkness obscured the rocky features in a blanket of shadow. Like death, the night had swallowed Abe's still form.

Younkin turned away. The canyon towered about him, estranged and alien. The escarpment's heights swirled before his eyes. His knees buckled, threatening to give way. The ground beneath his feet felt liquid, an undulating viscosity planted on solid earth. In the distance, he heard a low moan; its pained sorrow resonated through the hollowness of his chest. Seeking the sound's source, his gaze darted around to find nothing. The cry came from his own lips.

He closed his eyes and wiped a hand over his face. He drew in a long, steady breath and exhaled. The uneasy swaying continued. Abe's death, a single bullet, had shattered something. A chasm yawned open to rend the past from the present. He stood alone, stranded in a land that contained no place for him, a land populated by machines that rumbled along on wheels and flew through the air on fragile cloth wings. The Rangers, Clara, scouting, Abe—time and death had taken them all from him, abandoning him in a world that held no purpose. His ties to the present were severed.

Black Hand.

Younkin's head jerked up. His eyes focused on the canyon. He remembered. The Comanche still lived. One door to the past remained ajar, a door that had waited twenty-seven years to be closed. Hate raged outward to consume his emptiness.

Tightening their grasp on the Winchester, his hands swung the rifle's drooping muzzle upward to cover an attack. He started down the canyon in strides, long and deliberate.

One of the three would be waiting for him, stationed to defend an attack from the rear. Of this he had no doubt. It did not matter. He would take the brave, then the other. Last of all, he would watch Black Hand die. He owed that to Abe. He owed that to himself.

Ahead, his eyes probed the canyon's darkness. The moon that hung overhead could not cut the blackness around him. Its glow contorted the walls into grotesque shapes that might hide a Comanche within each of their shadows.

Nothing moved within the canyon, no hint of the brave he knew waited for him. Nor did he hear anything. He cocked his head to the side. No bird, animal, or insect moved through the night. The eerie silence gathered to press down on him.

"Damn," Younkin's steps hastened. Missing also was the sporadic exchange of rifle fire between his companions and the Comanches.

Rounding the canyon's sharp bend, he stared across the wide clearing. Moonlight played like frost over the three carcasses of the dead horses. He saw no sign of Black Hand or the two other braves.

Slower, hugging the shadow of the canyon wall, he edged around the clearing to its opposite end. He cocked the rifle and stepped from the shadows.

The canyon opened before, running to its narrow mouth. A quarter of a mile ahead of him stood the boulders that had held the Comanches. Nothing moved.

Black Hand and the two braves were gone.

Younkin stood in disbelief, unable to accept the scene that met his eyes.

The cracking report of rifle fire splintered the silence.

"Damn!" In that instant, Younkin understood. He stumbled forward in a trot, then broke into a full run.

CHAPTER 17

Toohmah methodically emptied his rifle into the backs of the unsuspecting Whites. Coolly, without the rage of bloodlust, he reloaded and once more emptied the weapon. To each side of him, Quinne and Chana knelt on one knee; blue-and-yellow blossoms of flame leaped from the muzzles of their rifles as they followed his lead.

Taken unawares, the white men twisted and jerked in a macabre dance, their forms dark silhouettes beneath the moonlight. Two of the men managed to swing their weapons toward the canyon's north wall and the shadows that cloaked the three Comanches. Each fired a single shot before the hail of lead cut him down. Their bullets whined off rock, an empty gesture in the face of death.

The old Comanche raised a hand, halting his young companions, who prepared to fire their reloaded rifles into the bodies that were strewn beside the outcropping of rock. There was no need to waste ammunition. The moon's soft glow revealed no movement among the Whites.

"We have done enough." Toohmah's stoic mask gentled to an expression of satisfaction. Their attack had come quick and heavy. He was not fool enough to believe all the Whites had been killed. The only way to be certain of that was to walk among them and place a bullet in each of their heads. To do that would be too dangerous. To leave the concealing shadows, to expose themselves, would be suicidal madness. A wounded man, even a dying one, can lift a rifle, aim, and squeeze a trigger.

Quinne and Chana rose. The latter's breath came heavy and uneven. Hidden in the darkness, Toohmah frowned. Perhaps his earlier praise for Chana had come too soon. Fear moved within the young man. His heart still was not one that belonged to a brave of the People.

"Uncle, the horses!" Quinne grabbed Toohmah's arm and pointed.

The Whites' horses had broken their tethers during the attack, frightened by the sudden gunfire and confusion. Scattered wildly across the gorge, they bolted toward the mouth of the canyon.

"Should we chase them?" Quinne questioned.

A low curse pushed its way over Toohmah's lips. He had wanted fresh mounts to replace those the Whites had killed. Now . . . he could not risk the chase. The satisfied expression faded from his face.

"We will go deeper in the canyon. Come." Pivoting, he started down the gorge in a loping run. Quinne and Chana followed at his heels.

The horses were not necessary; time was essential. The Whites would not stop, Toohmah realized. Even if they had killed all those by the outcropping, there would be others who would eventually take up the trail, their determination fired by the shame of repeated defeats at the hands of three lone Comanches. The white man's pride could not suffer that.

Toohmah hastened his strides. He would lead the others up the canyon wall. Once atop the caprock they would find a ranch and steal horses to carry them southward to the land of the *Mejanos*.

He smiled. Freedom in Mexico, that would be the supreme victory, to completely evade the Whites when he crossed the Rio Grande. He pushed the thought from his mind. Mexico lay too far in the distance. To walk the High Plains would be enough. It would be a victory that no White could ever conceive of. Were he to die the instant his feet touched the caprock's soil, he would have won what no man could snatch from him. Tomorrow morning, anticipation ran like lightning through his body, he would tread the High Plains.

His strides lengthened, the age of his legs melting away. The frailties of the flesh fled before his soaring spirit. The chase, the hunt, the attack, they fed his soul, fired the strength of his muscles. The years, the reservation, were meaningless. He was Comanche and a Blood Moon ruled the night sky.

A mile, perhaps two, from the outcropping, Toohmah had lost judgment of distance in the rush of exhilaration, he stopped after rounding a sharp bend in the canyon's wall. He smiled. A second bend lay but five hundred feet farther into Palo Duro. The second bend provided the shelter they needed for the night. In the morning, they would climb atop the caprock. If Younkin and any other Whites followed . . .

Younkin? Doubt, a possibility Toohmah did not wish to face, niggled at the back of his mind. Surely the scout lay dead with his companions . . . or wounded. Yet . . .

Toohmah walked toward the second bend, trying to shake the uneasiness that dampened his spirits. If Younkin had survived the attack, he would lead the Whites. Alone, if necessary, the scout would come after him. As surely as Toohmah would sacrifice his own life to kill this enemy come from the past, he knew Younkin would follow though his body were mortally wounded.

What drove such a man? The white man's years equaled his, yet Younkin was relentless in his pursuit. Did the man's hate equal the hate that the Comanche carried in his chest? For what? Toohmah shook his head, puzzled by the forces that worked within such a man.

"We'll camp here for the night." The thought of Younkin alive and behind him darkened his soul. He turned to his two companions. Only Quinne was there. He glanced at the son of his sister's daughter. "Chana?"

Quinne swirled around, searching for the third member of their band. He looked back at Toohmah. "He was right behind me."

The old man's uneasiness increased. "Wait here. I will go back and find him."

He started to retrace their steps, stopped, and looked back at Quinne. "If I do not return within the hour, climb the wall and flee to the south."

Not waiting for Quinne to question his instructions, Toohmah trotted off. Where his legs had seemed so strong but moments ago, they now carried the full weight of his age. Each step hurt, arthritic pain cutting into his knees. He grimaced, gritting his teeth.

A quarter of a mile from where he had left Quinne, he found Chana. The youth lay on his side close to the canyon wall. Both his hands clutched his stomach. Toohmah squatted beside him.

Chana's eyes opened. "You came back. The Whites . . . I'm hurt."

He removed his hands to reveal the dark wetness that covered their palms. Blood stained the front of the shirt he wore. It couldn't be. Toohmah had heard the ricochet of the Whites' bullets. It just couldn't be. Yet it was.

Against hope, Toohmah tore open the shirt. Like a second navel, the small bullet wound sat at the center of his belly. He had seen many young braves die from such wounds, knew the prolonged agony such a death brought. Yet Chana gave no outward display of pain.

"Am I dying?" A stream of blood flowed from one of the young man's nostrils.

"Yes." It never occurred to the older man to hide the truth. "Soon you will ride with the braves in the Valley of Ten Thousand-fold Longer and Wider. You will hunt and ride to war as befits a warrior."

"And the Whites?" Chana's voice was a soft whisper. "Will they hunt us there?"

"The valley is not for the Whites." Guilt coursed through the older man. He remembered Chana's ragged breaths after the attack. He had mistaken the younger man's heavy breathing for a sign of fear. A man could be no more wrong. Chana had contained the fire that devoured his entrails when other men would have screamed in fear and pain. Only the bravest of warriors held such strength. "You will ride with the mightiest of the People, and they will call you by the name Permero Okoom."

"Permero Okoom, the Bull. It is a good name." Chana coughed. Blood and phlegm sprayed from his lips. His face contorted as pain racked his body. "It wasn't supposed to end like this."

"It will be over shortly, then there will be no pain." Toohmah rested a hand on Chana's shoulder. "I will stay with you and see you on your journey."

The younger man did not answer. His eyes gazed vacantly out onto the canyon; his chest did not move. Toohmah leaned over. He felt no breath come from Chana's lips.

Mentally chanting a death song, the old brave rose. He grasped his dead companion by the arms and dragged him behind three fallen boulders. He then gathered rocks and covered the body. It was not a fitting grave for one so brave, but it was all he could offer the warrior as a final resting place.

"Permero Okoom," Toohmah whispered to his dead companion, then turned and began walking back to Quinne. *It wasn't supposed to end like this.* The youth's final words refused to leave his mind.

Chana's hopes had taken him to Mexico, where he would have spent his life in freedom. Now, he lay dead because of an old man's insistence on once again walking the land of his birth. Had Boisa Pah's dreams been different? He now lay dead, killed by the same old man's hunting knife. Toohmah's eyes closed tightly in an attempt to hold back the welling tears of guilt and anger.

No, Toohmah told himself. Both young men had been given the choice to ride with him or to make their own way to Mexico. They had made their decision and followed him. The choice had been theirs alone.

He deceived himself. There had been no choice. On their own, neither Chana nor Boisa Pah would have made it to the land of the *Mejanos*. They had been soft, unable to scrounge the land for food and shelter. They would not have survived for more than a few days before the Whites had ridden them down. Boisa Pah had seen that. His anger had stemmed from his frustration at being trapped by an old man.

Toohmah had given them but one choice, his way, the old way of the People. And they had died.

They had died!

A high-pitched wail of shame and mourning rose from the old man's throat and tore from his mouth, rising to the Moon Mother. The burden of the two deaths was his alone, bowing his shoulders with an unbearable weight.

Youth had died. He had tried to return to a world that no longer existed. Was that the old ways of the *Nermernuh*? Was that the way of old men, to kill the young? Did he harbor some jealousy for those who would inherit the land after his death?

He cursed himself and his blindness. The irony of the past months writhed and knotted within his gut. Three young men had come to him for aid, to draw upon the experience of his years. Had he provided the counsel that reflected the wisdom of those years? No, he had assumed leadership of the small band. The old never had led the People, that was reserved for the young whose lives remained before them. What war chief could truly claim success if he rode back to camp with the bodies of companions killed under his leadership?

The horror of what he had blindly done railed within him. There was no escape from the results of his greedy selfishness. He had placed his desires, those of a dried-up old man, above those of youth. His world was not the world of the son of his sister's daughter, nor was it that which had belonged to Chana and Boisa Pah. He had hoped to give them the world of his own youth, what had once been his. What use did they have of that? The world he now walked was theirs. He could never regain that which time had stripped away.

Glancing up as he rounded the canyon's first bend, Toohmah saw Quinne standing where he had ordered him to wait.

Waiting for what? Death.

The truth squirmed free within Toohmah's soul. He was death that walked on two feet. Death was all that awaited Quinne if he remained at the side of his grandmother's brother. Twice the old Comanche had killed his own people. Now he offered the same fate to one that carried his own blood. Had age made him so contemptuous of youth's vitality?

No! He refused to rob the son of his sister's daughter of the right to find his own world and life. He would lead Quinne from the canyon this very night. They would raid a ranch. With fresh horses they could reach Mexico within three days. It would be hard riding without sleep or food, but it could be done.

Toohmah caught himself. *Mexico?* What had seemed the way to a complete victory over the Whites but moments ago now seemed hollow and meaningless. Mexico held no place for him. This, the High Plains and Palo Duro, was his land, his world. It was all he had ever truly known. Mexico was but another reservation, the borders of which would hold him as surely as had the White guards at Fort Sill. Mexico could never offer him the peace he found here.

"Chana?" Quinne stared at his uncle. "Is he dead? I heard a wail of mourning."

"A belly wound. He died bravely." Toohmah nodded. His eyes rode up the full height of the canyon's wall. He could climb it with Quinne. But what would remain? There was no purpose in fleeing with Quinne. The son of his sister's daughter could fend for himself; he had learned much in the past months. There was a better use for the last moments of an old man. Something he could do to assuage the guilt he carried and aid Quinne's escape.

Toohmah's gaze returned to the young man. "You must prepare to go now. To stay would only mean death for you."

"We should rest before starting the climb. You are tired." Quinne stripped off his shirt and tied it to the muzzle and stock of his rifle, making a sling. He slipped it around head and shoulder.

"Only you will go. I stay." He reached into the saddlebags and produced two boxes of cartridges that he handed to Quinne. "The *nenuhpee* was right. The High Plains are not meant for me."

"Uncle, I will stay—" Quinne began.

"You will climb the canyon." The muzzle of Toohmah's rifle rose, leveled at the younger man's stomach. "Your arm will slow you, but there are handholds and footholds, enough for a child to make the climb. Go slowly and carefully. Once on the caprock find a ranch, steal a horse and ride to Mexico. You will be free there."

"Uncle, I have no wish to—" Quinne protested.

"Climb." Toohmah jabbed the youth's belly with the rifle. "In Mexico find a woman. When you have a child, remember me to him. Now climb."

Hesitantly, Quinne started up the sloping foot of the canyon wall. He stopped and turned back to his uncle. "I shall call my son Toohmah."

"Name him Cona cheak, the name given me by my father's brother. It is a good name," Toohmah answered.

Standing at the foot of the wall, Toohmah watched Quinne resume the climb. Cautiously, favoring his injured arm, the young man picked his way up the rocky face. Eventually, he crawled over the rim, vanishing for a moment. Then he was there again, standing, peering down at his uncle.

Toohmah raised his rifle high above his head and swung it to the south. Without a word, Quinne turned and walked away, disappearing behind the canyon's rim.

For a moment, the old man stood staring above at the place his sister's daughter's son had stood. He smiled. He had made the right choice; youth would live. He turned and started deeper into the canyon. When morning came, if it brought Younkin and other Whites, he would be waiting. He would delay their search, giving Quinne the time needed to make his way beyond the Texas border.

CHAPTER 18

Younkin reached the mouth of the tributary canyon and halted. His head cocked from left to right, straining to hear any sound that would provide an indication of what was happening within the main gorge. The vast chasm of Palo Duro Canyon stood silent, undisturbed by even the calls of nocturnal predators. Only the panicked throb of his pulse reverberated in the scout's ears.

Refusing to consider the implication contained within the stillness, Younkin lifted his rifle to his chest, ready to swing it into action, and stepped from behind the boulders. The pounding of his heart grew louder. Dread constricted his chest. Nothing moved around the outcropping of rock that shielded his companions.

A clack of stones sounded behind him. Younkin swirled, the barrel of the Winchester leveled to meet an attack.

In a shadowy blur of motion, a jackrabbit scurried across the canyon floor. The scout cursed softly to himself as he peered westward into Palo Duro's depths. Nothing.

He swung back to the outcropping and slowly began to walk. From shadow to shadow, his gaze darted; an imagined Comanche hid within each. No attack came.

Slinking to a crouched walk, he approached the outcrop of limestone. No sound issued from behind the barrier of rock. Fear pressed across his rib cage like taut leather straps. There was no doubt now. Black Hand had used the night to attack, overwhelming his son and the other men. He held no hope that any of the six lived. The only question that remained was, were Black Hand and his braves waiting behind the limestone?

The answer came in the distinct metallic clicking of a pistol being cocked.

Younkin reacted rather than thought. He leaped from behind the outcropping and hit the ground in a roll. A single shot exploded, its report ripping through the silence. Sand showered the side of the scout's face as the bullet spent itself in the ground mere inches from its target.

Determined to deny the attacker a second, more accurate shot, Younkin came to his knees, the Winchester's barrel homing in on the chest of the man who stood above him. The scout hesitated; his finger uncurled around the trigger.

"You?" Lieutenant Bishop's voice drifted to him in a puzzled whisper. The revolver he held lowered. "I thought you were one of *them* come back to finish the job they started. I thought they had killed you, too."

The army officer sank to the sand and sat there. The pistol fell from his fingers. He stared blankly at the older man.

"Pa?" Tom called, his voice weak and strained. "Is that you, Pa?"

Younkin pushed from the ground. A gasp caught and lodged in his throat. Private Michael Woebbe, Deputy Hank Wells, George Pilgrim, Haas's saloon owner, and Marvin Browder, the town's blacksmith, lay sprawled in the dirt where they had fallen beneath the Comanches' hail of bullets. The sand darkened in wet pools about their bodies.

Younkin glanced away from the carnage. Somehow, beneath the horror of the moment, his mind registered the fact that the horses were gone.

"Pa?"

Younkin's gaze shifted to his son who sat propped against a boulder. That same dark wetness spread over the right side of his chest. Stepping over the bodies of his dead companions, Younkin knelt beside his son.

"Bishop was going to find the horses and Woebbe's medical

kit when we heard your footsteps." Tom paused; his gaze pushed past Younkin. "Where's Abe?"

"Dead," Younkin replied tersely as he unbuttoned his son's shirt and folded back the fabric.

"Bad?" Tom looked at his father, his face a reflection of the young boy who had grown to a man at Younkin's side.

"It's a long way from your heart." Younkin closed the shirt, unable to determine the extent of the wound. "You could do with some bandaging. I'll see if I can find the horses."

"What about the lieutenant?" Tom's question ended as his face contorted in pain.

"I'll take care of Bishop." Younkin placed his hand on his son's shoulder. "You lay here and rest. Understand?"

Tom nodded. Younkin glanced at the officer, noticing the dark, wet stain on the shoulder of his uniform. Bishop's head rose to the scout, then his neck craned so that he looked down at the wound. His gaze came back to Younkin. "It can wait. The bleeding's stopped."

"The horses?"

Bishop's head tilted toward the entrance of the canyon. "The shots frightened them. They ran toward the east. After the attack, the Comanches went deeper into the canyon. It . . . they . . . I . . . ," the officer stammered, then sat silently.

"I'll be back as soon as I can." Younkin rose, rifle in hand and started toward Palo Duro's mouth.

Less than a quarter of a mile from the limestone outcropping, he found the horses grazing. Locating his mount, he approached it with cautious steps, afraid any sudden movement would spook the animals. The bay's head rose once to eye him, then lowered back to the grass. Inching closer, Younkin carefully extended an arm and snared the horse's loose reins.

He ran a calming hand along the animal's broad neck and mounted. With no difficulty, he weaved among the other horses and found Woebbe's and Tom's mounts. Gathering their reins, he turned back toward the outcropping.

The attack never should have occurred. Younkin brooded, unable to dislodge the vision of his slain friends and companions. If not Bishop, then Tom should have realized Black Hand would make a move once night provided a cloak for his actions. Bishop with his military methods, and Tom and his progress, had both been robbed of simple common sense? Comanches loved the night; it held no supernatural fear for them as it did with other tribes. Tom and Bishop should have known . . .

His logic faltered. How could they have known? Neither the army officer nor his son had been alive when the Comanches terrorized the Texas frontier with their constant Blood Moon raids. Only one man among the eight who had ridden after Black Hand fully understood the Comanche's wiles and abilities. That man was Jess Younkin.

Guilt and shame bent his shoulders. Abe and four others lay dead, and Bishop and Tom were wounded, because he had been careless. Had he been less anxious to drive Black Hand into a corner, there never would have been an attack. Had he warned his son and the officer of the possibilities. Had he not been so eager to prove himself capable of succeeding where younger men had failed.

Since the manhunt began, he had cursed Bishop and Tom for their lack of confidence in his ability. Now that he had attained that trust, what had he given them? Five dead men, five men lost because of his stupidity. Five men dead because of an old man's foolish pride.

And he had almost killed Tom. The horror of what might have occurred quaked through him to leave his hands shaking and his knees watery. Only luck had saved him from the disgrace and irreplaceable loss.

His heels jabbed the bay's flanks, urging it to a faster pace. Black Hand belonged to neither Bishop nor Tom. The Comanche was his, had always been his. Why had he required disaster to accept that?

Upon reaching the limestone outcropping, Younkin dismounted, tied the horses' reins to a young cedar, then took Woebbe's medical kit from the dead soldier's saddlebags. He lifted a canteen from his saddle horn and walked to Tom.

Gingerly, he opened his son's shirt and cleansed the bullet

wound. Covering the purple-tinged hole with antiseptic powder, he wrapped Tom's chest in a tight bandage.

"Pa, how bad is it?" Tom reached out to grasp his father's wrist as the older man rose.

"It'll be all right." Younkin did not like the sound of his son's labored breathing. A wet rasping gurgled in his throat. The bullet had missed Tom's heart, but had struck a lung. Younkin could only hope the internal bleeding was minimal. "I'd feel better if a doctor took a look at you."

"It's hard to breathe. Can't get enough air." Tom grimaced. "Feels like someone's sitting on my chest."

"It'll get better. Just rest and don't try to move." The wound would not get better without a physician's care, Younkin realized. He hid his fear with a smile and a firm squeeze to his son's shoulder when he stood.

The old scout crossed to where Bishop sat staring into Palo Duro's darkness. The officer looked up at the older man, his head moving from side to side. "We didn't see them leave the rocks. They were firing at us before we knew they were there. It was like a meat grinder, bullets bouncing off the rocks. We couldn't get away."

"Let me take a look at the shoulder." Younkin waited until the lieutenant unbuttoned his blouse. He bent close and washed the wound. "You're lucky. It's a deep crease, but nothing serious."

Bishop winced as Younkin sprinkled powder over the raw wound. "Tom?"

"Bad," Younkin whispered so his son could not hear. "He needs a doctor. I want you to take him to Clarendon. It's about thirty miles east of—"

"Black Hand?" Bishop stared up in disbelief. "I can't leave. I've got to track down Black Hand and his braves."

"A wounded man's no good to me." Younkin shook his head while he bandaged the shoulder. "You can't hold a rifle with this arm."

"But—" Bishop tried to protest.

"No buts. If you leave now, you can have Tom with a doctor by morning. If you don't, he'll be dead." Younkin gave the lieutenant directions to the small town while he rebuttoned his shirt. "Gather a couple guns and I'll get Tom."

While Bishop did as directed, Younkin lifted his son to his feet, then half-carried him to his mount. Using a shoulder, he pushed Tom up into the saddle and then turned to his bay and mounted. When Bishop joined them, the three reined toward the canyon's mouth. Younkin's gaze hung on his son, searching for any hint that the wound had reopened. There was none. Tom was weak, but he managed to remain in the saddle.

As they approached the horses still grazing within the canyon, Younkin guided the bay beside a black mare and took her reins. The extra horse would serve as a pack animal on which to carry the bodies of Black Hand and his braves. The scout turned to Bishop. "Don't try to push it. Ride slow and easy, and you should be in Clarendon by morning. I think Tom can make it. But if the bleeding starts again, stop." He handed Bishop the medical kit. "This is where I leave you."

"What?" Tom's head snapped up with the realization of what his father intended. "Pa, you can't go after them alone!"

Younkin wheeled the bay around without a glance at his son. There was no time for an argument. He clucked the horse to a trot.

"Pa?" Tom called after him. "Pa?"

Younkin tried to blot out the sound of his son's voice. He had done all he could for Tom. It was up to Lieutenant Bishop now, and the doctor in Clarendon.

A half-mile beyond the limestone outcropping, Younkin stopped. He had pushed his luck enough for one night, he decided. Ahead of him, three Comanches lay in wait. They could be hiding in any shadow, behind any rock. The morning's light would make the tracking easy.

He glanced from one side of the canyon to the other. On the left, he found a clump of mesquite, cedar and scrub oak. A hundred feet above the dense vegetation, on the canyon's wall, three boulders pushed from the sandy soil.

Moving to the trees, Younkin slid from the saddle, tied the

horses to an oak branch, and stripped them of their saddles. Saddle blankets under his left arm and rifle securely clutched in his right hand, the scout scrambled up the wall's gentle incline to the boulders. He surveyed his surroundings. The position was perfect. The horses were visible, as was the canyon's gorge for a quarter of a mile in either direction.

Younkin stepped behind the boulders and kicked aside the larger stones in the sand with the side of a boot. Rolling one blanket for a pillow, he lowered himself to the ground and covered his chest with the remaining blanket. Rifle at his side, he smiled. The boulders provided a barrier that blocked the northerly breeze that blew in over the canyon's rim.

He closed his eyes to clear his mind of everything that had happened in the past few hours. Abe, the attack, his careless mistakes, nothing was to be gained by dwelling on them. After he had dealt with Black Hand, there would be time for mourning and sifting through the emotions and doubts that ate at him. Until then, he needed to keep his thoughts straight, focused on the task at hand.

After I finish what I've got to do, he told himself, *then* . . .

Jennifer Steele's image floated behind his closed eyelids. Those were the exact words he had spoken to her. A smile played over his lips as he fixed the delicate features of the woman's face in his mind's eye. The night they had shared had been good. After Clara's death, he had never lain with another woman. He had convinced himself he was too old to feel what Jenny had awakened in him that night.

And she waited for him to return. Together, they would make a life, working a small section of the ranch. With a few head of cattle and maybe a vegetable garden, they could . . .

Jenny's image dissipated. He lied to himself. He had lied to Jenny. Her offer was more than he had ever hoped for, but it was one he never would accept. Working stock and tilling the soil belonged to other men. He had not been cut out to be a farmer or a rancher. He had learned that in East Texas after Clara and his wedding. They would have starved to death, if the Rangers had not accepted him. No, he was not a rancher. He was a . . .

He was not sure what he was. He had been a soldier, a scout, a Ranger, and a lawman. Was any of those a profession a man could build a lifetime on?

There was the livery stable. That was another self-deception. The stable had been Abe's. With the right partner, Abe would have made it work. He had had a grasp of business. His friend had been right, Younkin admitted to himself. He saw the stable as a tombstone, a monument of straw and manure to mark the end of his life. He had never tried to make a success of the stable.

Damn! He cursed himself, the man he now perceived as Jess Younkin. Despite the weeks of tracking, despite the senseless killing, despite Abe's death, he was at peace with himself. This was the only life he had ever known. There was nothing else for him.

He now understood why he had been unable to kill Black Hand that night at the arroyo. The Comanche provided him the only opportunity left to live as he once had.

Tom was right, too. He was out of step with the world. Once he had been needed, then the country changed, leaving him behind. He had done nothing to keep pace, nor had he wanted to. These past weeks, he had selfishly sought to return to his past.

The price of that selfishness, Abe's death—and perhaps Tom's. The image of his son slumped in the saddle filled his head. The cost had been too high, too precious.

Tomorrow he would finally close the remaining door to his past that stood ajar. Then he would reenter the world around him.

CHAPTER 19

February 5, 1904

The early-morning cold brought Toohmah shivering from a shallow sleep haunted by dreams of his first days on the reservation. He lay motionless, listening, peering through slitted eyes to assure himself that only the chilled air was responsible for disturbing his troubled rest. Other than a constant wind that blew from the north, nothing stirred about him.

The *Nermernuh* shoved from the ground to shake off the residue of the disquieting dreams. The sudden movement was a mistake. He groaned. Hot nails drove into the joints of his body to awaken the throbbing pain of arthritis. Slowly now, he stretched his stiff limbs. Disregarding the pain in his fingers, he rubbed and kneaded his calves and thighs until he could flex his legs with no more than needlelike twinges.

While he massaged life back into his arms, Toohmah scanned the blue-gray pre-dawn sky. No clouds drifted overhead to blot out the last stars of night, yet the air was moisture laden. The false spring of the past weeks had died during the night, he realized. The winter would return in its full howling strength before sunset. The moisture and cold would combine to bring snow to Palo Duro.

The aged brave shivered. An unprotected man would not survive the coming storm. He remembered the buffalo robe tied to the saddle abandoned in the tributary canyon, longing for the moth-eaten fur to warm his bare shoulders.

From the saddlebags beside him on the ground, he extracted a black woolen shirt and slipped it on. He left the baggy white man's trousers within. They provided no more protection from the cold than his leggings and would restrict movement should he have to make a hasty retreat from his position.

Next, he took two boxes of cartridges from the leather bags and set them at his feet. When and if they were needed, the spare bullets lay within easy reach.

A low rumble that mounted to a loud, angry growl rolled through his belly. His hand rummaged through the saddlebags, seeking a forgotten portion of jerky. Toohmah's hand withdrew, empty. His stomach protested again. He ignored it. There was nothing else he could do.

Lifting his rifle, he double-checked to make certain it was fully loaded, then rested the weapon on his crossed legs. His gaze rose up the canyon wall to the rim above. Loneliness filled his breast. Had Quinne found a rancher's horse? Did he now ride to Mexico and freedom? The aged warrior refused to consider the alternatives; they would rob his decision to remain within Palo Duro of its purpose, its meaning.

He shivered again. The canyon appeared distant and alien this morning. Gone were yesterday's comforting memories. Palo Duro was but an eroded abyss of rock and sand that no longer held a place for the *Nermernuh*. The Comanches were a dead nation. The land was a living thing that brought forth life each spring. It had no use for the dead, except to absorb their flesh and bones to fertilize the grass and trees.

Toohmah looked eastward, unable to shed the darkness that shadowed his spirit. The Sun Father lifted his fiery body above the horizon. The lone brave reached down and cocked his rifle. And he waited.

The sun woke Younkin. He pushed to his elbows with a disgusted grunt. He had not meant to sleep this late. He glanced to the horses standing undisturbed, tethered to the scrub oak. The scout sat up and rubbed his arms. The morning's chill penetrated to the bone, despite his fleece-lined coat. Wind gusted over the canyon's rim, its icy breath nipping at the exposed flesh of his face. He cursed. The unseasonably warm spell had ended; winter had returned. The air carried a warning of an approaching blue norther.

Younkin shuddered when he stood and picked the saddle blankets from the ground. Palo Duro was no place for a man during a blizzard. Last winter, three hunters had been trapped in the canyon's rocky maze when a snowstorm struck. They had frozen to death before they could find their way out of the immense gorge.

Rifle and blankets in arm, Younkin carefully picked his way down the sandy incline. Reaching the horses, he saddled the bay and left the black mare bareback. Dead men needed no saddles, and he intended to bring the Comanches out of Palo Duro dead.

From a saddlebag, he took his remaining box of cartridges, emptying it into his coat pockets. When he located Black Hand, there would be no time to search for ammunition. Checking that the Winchester carried a full load, Younkin mounted the bay. He then reached down and untethered the mare's reins. Rifle in the crook of his left arm and leading the mare with his right, he clucked the bay forward.

Wind-whipped dust and sand raked across the gorge. Here and there, dust devils swirled like miniature tornadoes, leaves and grass caught in the whirling columns. Younkin paid them no heed, his gaze constantly surveying the canyon's walls.

A mile from the boulders that had sheltered him in the night, he sighted four low-circling buzzards. Below them, along the foot of the south wall, he saw the pile of rocks partially hidden behind three boulders.

Dismounting, he removed three of the larger stones. A pleased, mirthless smile curled his lips as he gazed down on the face of the brave buried under the rocks. The odds had suddenly improved. Only two Comanches awaited him up the canyon.

Younkin replaced the rocks to keep scavengers away from the body until his return. He then found a dried oak branch and drove a jagged end into the ground to mark the burial site. Even in heavy snow, he would be able to locate the marker.

Younkin searched the ground around the grave and shook

his head. Any tracks left by the Comanches last night were gone now. His own bootprints were quickly erased by the wind. A trail would have made things easier, but it was of no consequence. Black Hand and the remaining brave were ahead of him, and he eventually would find them.

Younkin walked back to the horses and climbed into the saddle. His eyes roved over the gorge. Nothing. He nudged the bay forward.

Toohmah squinted against the morning, his eyes low to avoid the blindness that came from staring into the face of the Sun Father. He had not considered the sunrise when he selected the position, but there was nothing he could do to escape the glare. The Whites would come out of the east, and he had to face them. He would win Quinne the time necessary to escape into the land of the *Mejanos.*

The old brave's eyes widened; his heart raced in a thudding rhythm. Adrenaline coursed through the *Nermernuh*'s veins.

A horse and rider rounded a bend in the canyon four hundred yards from the boulders that concealed the Comanche. The White led a bareback horse beside him.

Toohmah resisted the impulse to lift his rifle and squeeze off a quick round. Others could be with the man. Better to catch them all by surprise.

The lone rider covered half the distance to the aged warrior, and still no other Whites followed. Toohmah's gaze narrowed. *Younkin!* Even at the distance, he discerned the scout's age-ravaged features. A smile eased over the Comanche's lips while he lifted his rifle to his shoulder. Only Younkin had survived last night's attack: one White man between him and the freedom that awaited beyond the canyon's rim. He took a bead on the rider's chest. His finger curled about the trigger and squeezed.

Younkin felt the shudder run through the bay before his mind registered the rifle's report. The black mare reared and wheeled, wrenching her reins from his grip. In full stride, she ran back toward the mouth of the canyon.

The bay stumbled. Vainly, Younkin attempted to kick free of the stirrups and leap from the saddle. The horse dropped from under him, rolling to its side. The scout went down, right leg pinned beneath the dying animal's ponderous weight.

The exploding sound of rifle fire echoed through the gorge. Sand flew into the air as bullets hammered into the ground in front of the trapped scout.

Squirming, kicking, Younkin wrenched at his leg to dislodge it from beneath the bay. Pain lanced through his foot like liquid fire. Gritting his teeth, he pulled; inch by inch the leg worked free.

Bullets peppering the ground about him, he sighted the dropped Winchester. He pushed to his feet. Agony seared white-hot through his right foot and ankle. They gave way beneath his weight, throwing him back to the ground. *Broken!* The foot and ankle were broken.

He moved rather than waste time on a curse. On hands and knees, he scrambled to the Winchester, then rolled behind a low mound of sand and talus at the foot of the canyon's south wall. Flat on his stomach, he pressed close to the sand, trying to sink below its surface. The din of rifle fire abruptly died. Apparently the pile of dirt and stone hid him from his attacker.

Attacker! The realization of what he had thought came to him. There had been only one rifle firing. He faced but one Comanche. He smiled, despite the desperation of his position. It was Black Hand out there. He knew it. The other brave had either been killed last night or had deserted the old Comanche when he recognized Palo Duro's dangers.

Younkin lifted his head. Six hundred feet in front of him, sunlight reflected off a single rifle barrel poked over a boulder. The scout ducked back as a howling gust of wind threw sand into his face. He blinked, clearing his eyes.

Scooting to his side, Younkin cocked the Winchester and edged its barrel atop the talus mound. He glanced up. Clouds, like massive black mountains in the sky, moved in from the north. He could almost feel the temperature dropping degree by degree. The norther was upon them. Little time remained until it unleashed its frozen fury.

Yonkin sighted along the rifle's barrel with a curse. He

could not get a clear shot at the Comanche. The boulders provided too much cover. For the moment, their positions presented a stalemate.

Peering over the stony pile, Younkin called out in the Comanche tongue. "Toohmah, the time of running is over. There is no more time for you. Soon the soldiers will come and you will die. The time of red man fighting white man is long passed. Surrender and you will be returned to the reservation unharmed."

Younkin's lie reverberated through the canyon. The old *Nermernuh* smiled while he reloaded his rifle. A hangman's rope awaited him at the reservation. His gaze played over the canyon. Thirty feet to his right lay a rounded boulder with a bushlike cedar growing before it.

He looked back to Younkin's position. The scout was wrong. While either of them lived, there was still time for fighting. Perhaps here, alone within Palo Duro, they would fight the last battle. If so, it was fitting that he face the scout. Of all the enemies Toohmah had faced, red, black, and white, none evoked the hate he held for Younkin. None had provided the satisfaction he would feel when he killed the man. That the scout lived after all these years proved his greatness and power. No man could ask for more than that in an adversary.

Toohmah's head turned back to the cedar-hidden boulder, his mind formulating a plan. Before the day was out, he would prove his own might by taking the man's scalp.

Younkin's voice rolled up to him, again demanding his surrender. With a high-pitched, yapping war cry, Toohmah pushed to his feet and fired two rapid shots toward the rocks that hid the scout. Then he darted toward the cedar.

Younkin saw the blur of movement. His finger squeezed the trigger, firing on instinct rather than taking a clear sight on his target.

Black Hand twisted in midair under the bullet's impact. He hit the ground, dropping behind a bushy cedar. *Dead?* Younkin fired three rounds into the evergreen. The shots whined off solid rock. The scrubby tree concealed a boulder.

If the Comanche lived, he now held a vantage point to pick Younkin off. The scout's gaze ran over the canyon. The dead bay's body offered the only close cover. He hesitated in making a move, unsure whether the Comanche lived or not.

Something cold and wet fluttered against Younkin's cheeks. He glanced up. Snow. In light flurries, it fell from the cloud-darkened sky. Time was running out. He had to do something. His head moved back to the bay's body.

Huddled behind the boulder, Toohmah cut a sleeve from his black shirt. Snowflakes in ever-increasing numbers pelted his exposed skin to melt and run in icy rivulets. He lifted his right leg. Blood oozed from the round bullet hole high on the interior of his left thigh. He wrapped the sleeve tautly about the wound and tied it in a knot. Later he would give it the care it required. Now, there was Younkin.

"Toohmah, I know I hit you." Younkin's voice eddied up the canyon. "There is no time left for fighting. Surrender and I will tend your wounds."

"*Tejano*, your aim has not lessened with the years," the *Nermernuh* called back. "Were I a younger man, I would now be worried about my ability to please a woman and produce sons. Since I am old, I have no such worries."

Toohmah leaned on a side and pushed his rifle's barrel through the dense cedar limbs. He cursed the gods who had forsaken him. Younkin still was not visible.

"Come tend my wound, *tohobaka* . . . then I will tend your grave," Toohmah continued. "It will give me great pride to kill such an old enemy."

Broken foot or not, Younkin had to run for the bay. He could not wait until the Comanche started shooting. In a crouch, he pushed upward. His right ankle flared with burning pain, but it held him: sprained, not broken. He hobble-ran for the horse.

The old brave's rifle barked. Searing and heavy, the shot hammered into Younkin's left shoulder. He staggered under the impact, then stumbled forward to fall behind the bay. Two more shots rang out. He felt them thud harmlessly into the horse's carcass.

"Now we are equal," Toohmah shouted. "We both carry the other's mark."

"No Comanche is my equal!" Younkin grimaced. His blood felt hot as it flowed from the wound and spread down his chest. He glanced to the cedar. Black Hand remained hidden. "The Comanches are snakes that I grind under my bootheel."

Laughter echoed off the canyon's walls. Toohmah answered, "No, Younkin, we are equals. We are the same man wearing skins of different colors . . ."

Younkin groaned as he wedged a hand inside his coat and shirt to press a handkerchief to the shoulder wound. His eyes batted, trying to keep the snow that swept into the canyon from them.

". . . Our time is past, Younkin. The world no longer holds us in its open palms. We have been turned away from life. Only death awaits us, but it is too slow in coming. Here, within the canyon, we have hastened death to us."

"I'll hasten your death, you bastard!" Younkin called back.

Again the old Comanche laughed. "And I yours. What more could men such as you and I ask for than to die at the hands of their oldest and mightiest enemy? Among my people, a man is measured by the strength of his enemies."

Black Hand's insane words resonated within Younkin. They shared more than each other's wounds. He tried to shake off the barrage of thoughts that assailed his mind, but they persisted, forcing him to confront their truths. What place was there for the Comanche in a world that spawned horseless carriages and flying machines? Nor did it offer a niche for a man whose abilities it no longer needed.

Younkin wiped melting snow from his face. Black Hand had escaped the reservation to find a world that had died twenty-eight years ago. For Younkin, the old brave's trail provided the road to a time that had been stolen from him when the people of Haas stripped away his badge.

Beyond the difference in red and white, past the years of hate that had molded them, they were like mirror reflections of one another. They were but two old men seeking a life that no longer existed, a time when they both understood the world that surrounded them. The kinship was inescapable.

"Measure a man by his enemy's strength?" Younkin called

out, sensing the tangled twines that had interwoven their lives through the years. "Then I am the mightiest of men!"

"And I." Toohmah grinned. He could barely see the fallen horse through the cascading snow. A coat of white covered the gorge's floor. Along the canyon's south wall, the wind whipped the fluffy whiteness into thick drifts.

"All things must end," he heard Younkin shout. "If we do not end the fighting, we will both die in the storm. Surrender, and I will see that no harm comes to you."

Toohmah heard the sincerity in the scout's voice, but what could one old man do to protect him from the soldiers? The aged *Nermernuh* shook his head. He would not, could not, return to the reservation and the blue-coated guards. His spirit would not be confined again; these brief weeks of freedom had been too sweet. "No, Younkin. The fighting will end when one of us lies dead. Then the snow will claim the one who remains. Such is the way brave enemies should die, on a battlefield with honor. It is a good day for dying, Younkin. Come, let me bring yours."

"The mare . . . the one that bolted down the canyon," Younkin answered. "She can carry one of us from Palo Duro. She can't have gone far."

Younkin paused, his mind racing. He had no intention of freezing to death while they both waited to pick the other off. There was a chance to end the standoff, a slim one, and it was weighted in his favor. Black Hand had never faced a man one-to-one with only his gun to back him. He had.

"Face me, Toohmah," Younkin challenged him. "Crawl out from behind your rock and face me like a man. The one who lives will have the mare to ride out on."

Warrior to warrior, alone on the battlefield; Toohmah nodded his silent approval. The scout offered him the chance he wanted, the opportunity to kill the man who had butchered his wife and child. If he failed?

There would be no shame in such a death. It would be the death of a *Nermernuh* brave, not an old man rotting on the white man's reservation. He tested his left leg against the ground. Pain erupted anew through the thigh, but it would support him.

"Stand and face me, Younkin," Toohmah answered the challenge. "Stand and face the brave who brings you death!"

Younkin crawled to his knees, his temples apound with the sound of his pulse. Through the falling veil of white, he saw Black Hand's form rise and step from behind the cedar. At last, he would close the door to his past. When it was over, he would . . .

His thoughts faltered as old doubts crept into his mind: the fear, always the fear. *No,* he told himself, feeling the fear flow from his body, replaced by an inner serenity. The snows would make a cleaner tombstone than the straw and manure that waited in the stable.

Younkin rose, standing full height. He held his rifle muzzle down at his side. Black Hand limped toward him in a lop-sided gait. The Comanche's rifle hung at his side.

Squinting against the falling snow, Younkin stepped around the dead bay. His gaze focused on the brave's rifle for any indication of movement.

Black Hand's barrel inched upward, as though he hoped to raise the weapon without Younkin's noticing. The scout swung the Winchester up in one fluid motion. His finger tightened about the trigger. A single shot blasted, its roar tearing through the howl of the wind.

Black Hand staggered back a half-step. He swayed, his body shuddering. Without a sound, he collapsed into the whiteness.

Rifle cocked for another shot, Younkin lifted the barrel and trained it on the still form. He waited, a minute, two, unwilling to approach the brave until he was certain no life remained within his ancient frame. Black Hand did not stir. A pink hue seeped from beneath his body to tint the snow around his chest. Younkin moved forward in short, cautious steps.

Fire and ice; fire raged in the *Nermernuh's* chest while ice caressed his flesh. He felt his bowels and bladder relax, emptying themselves as death approached. A silent curse worked

M50

from his mouth, voicelessly spoken to the snow. Fortune had chosen to honor the scout. The double-edged blade of the *nenuhpee* had fallen. Soon his life's blood would drain from his heart. There had never been a means to escape his vision, never.

A weak smile touched Toohmah's lips. The Valley of Ten Thousand-fold Longer and Wider waited for him. The spirits of long-dead companions gathered there to greet him. How glorious the reunion would be if he could boast of sending his mightiest enemy to the pits of the white man's hell.

He sensed rather than felt the rifle within his numb hand. He sucked at the air, but it evaded him, refusing to fill his lungs with its strength. It did not matter. He struggled against the river of fire and ice that sought to sweep him away to lift himself on an elbow. The trembling barrel of his rifle rose to center on the manlike form that approached through the falling white. His finger curled around the trigger and pulled.

The slug slammed into the center of Younkin's chest. He stumbled backward. In an involuntary reaction, his finger squeezed. The rifle fired. Black Hand's head snapped back, a shower of red splattering over the snow. Then, he lay motionless in the cold, white carpet once again.

Amid the pain, Younkin struggled to keep his eyes open. *Damn!* He had not seen the old brave move, and he had been staring at him. Had it been the snow? Had he blinked? *Damn!* He hurt. But he still lived. He took a step forward, his boot finding only open air. He collapsed facedown in the snow.

Through the tearing agony that rent his chest, Younkin swam to lift his head. Black Hand did not move. His last shot had finished the brave, had closed that last door. The saline taste of blood filled his mouth when he tried to smile. *Damn!*

Gathering his strength, he attempted to rise. All he managed was to twist his head to the side. In the distance, he saw his hand, still clutching the Winchester. Slowly he released the weapon, his fingers sliding from it. His palm opened to the sky. Snowflakes pelted down to cover his hand. Younkin closed his eyes, surrendering to the comforting numbness of the cold, allowing the snow to cover him in its white blanket.